"You tempt me, Janice.

"The way your lips curl into a smile, with your quiet confidence, your gentle way with your children. I have no right to give in to that temptation. No right at all."

"And if I gave you that right?"

Unable to help himself, Logan touched her cheek with his fingertips. "That would be a gift I couldn't accept no matter how much I might want to. Not now."

"You mean because Ray hasn't been dead long—"

"You're vulnerable. I don't want to take advantage of you."

Janice exhaled a tiny sigh. "You seem to think I'll do something rash, as if being widowed is to be let out of a bottle, sure I'll do something foolish."

"Would you?"

"With you? Very possibly."

Dear Reader,

Every month Harlequin American Romance brings you four powerful men, and four admirable women who know what they want—and go all out to get it. Check out this month's sparkling selection of love stories, which you won't be able to resist.

First, our AMERICAN BABY promotion continues with Kara Lennox's *Baby by the Book*. In this heartwarming story, a sexy bachelor comes to the rescue when a pretty single mother goes into labor. The more time he spends with mother and child, the more he finds himself wanting the role of dad....

Also available this month is *Between Honor and Duty* by Charlotte Maclay, the latest installment in her MEN OF STATION SIX series. Will a firefighter's determination to care for his friend's widow and adorable brood spark a vow to love, honor and cherish? Next, JUST FOR KIDS, Mary Anne Wilson's miniseries continues with an office romance between *The C.E.O. & the Secret Heiress*. And in *Born of the Bluegrass* by Darlene Scalera, a woman is reunited with the man she never stopped loving—the father of her secret child.

Enjoy this month's offerings, and be sure to return each and every month to Harlequin American Romance!

Wishing you happy reading,

Melissa Jeglinski
Associate Senior Editor
Harlequin American Romance

BETWEEN HONOR AND DUTY

Charlotte Maclay

HARLEQUIN®

TORONTO • NEW YORK • LONDON
AMSTERDAM • PARIS • SYDNEY • HAMBURG
STOCKHOLM • ATHENS • TOKYO • MILAN • MADRID
PRAGUE • WARSAW • BUDAPEST • AUCKLAND

Special thanks to the men and women of the Torrance Fire Department and to all emergency personnel who risk their lives to protect the rest of us.

ISBN 0-373-16894-2

BETWEEN HONOR AND DUTY

Visit us at www.eHarlequin.com

Printed in U.S.A.

ABOUT THE AUTHOR

Charlotte Maclay can't resist a happy ending. That's why she's had such fun writing more than twenty titles for Harlequin American Romance and Harlequin Duets, plus several Silhouette Romance books, as well. Particularly well known for her volunteer efforts in her hometown of Torrance, California, Charlotte says her philosophy is that you should make a difference in your community. She and her husband have two married daughters and two grandchildren, whom they are occasionally allowed to baby-sit. She loves to hear from readers and can be reached at: P.O. Box 505, Torrance, CA 90501.

Books by Charlotte Maclay

HARLEQUIN AMERICAN ROMANCE

WHO'S WHO AT FIRESTATION SIX

Logan Strong—This dedicated firefighter finds it takes more courage to follow his heart than to enter a burning building.

Janice Gainer—If she takes a second chance on love, will she betray the past?

Kevin Gainer—Since the death of his father, Janice's nine-year-old son has become the man of the house... and he takes his job as "protector" very seriously.

Maddie Gainer—Kevin's six-year-old sister considers her big brother to be a hero like her dad.

Harlan Gray—The dedicated fire chief will go to the wall for his men; the only thing he can't do is escape a pursuing councilwoman.

Councilwoman Evie Anderson—Has her eye on the most eligible widower in town, Chief Gray.

Emma Jean Witowsky—The dispatcher has an uncanny way of predicting the future—especially when it comes to matters of the heart.

Tommy Tonka—An adolescent genius in all things mechanical, but he needs help from his firefighter friends when it comes to girls.

Mack Buttons—The station mascot, a five-year-old chocolate dalmatian who loves kids, people and the men of Station Six.

Chapter One

He couldn't stay away any longer.

It had been a month since the warehouse fire that had cost Ray Gainer his life. Now Logan Strong was en route to his widow's house in a tract of homes on the outskirts of Paseo del Real in central California. He'd never be able to tell her or her kids the truth about what had happened that day. He wasn't going to destroy the heroic legacy Ray had left behind when death had claimed the city's firefighter.

But Logan owed Janice Gainer something. And Ray's kids, too. If he'd acted on his instincts that morning, Ray never would have died. Janice wouldn't be a widow, the kids would have a father.

The truth twisted in Logan's gut. He'd vowed to bury the knowledge of what had happened that morning six feet under the ground along with Ray's remains. Being a firefighter meant you were part of a closed fraternity. You didn't blow the whistle on a brother, particularly when your brother's own stupidity had let the red devil claim his life.

Maybe, if he handled it right, Logan could help Janice's transition from wife to widow with the least pain for all concerned. Despite what had happened, he owed Ray that much. It didn't matter that Logan had trouble looking the men of Station Six in the eye these days, afraid he'd give the truth away.

He'd never forget that he shouldn't have allowed Ray to go up on the warehouse roof in the first place, or forgive himself. That was his failing—not listening to his own instincts.

He parked his Mustang at the curb in front of a two-story stucco house with a Spanish tile, fire-resistant roof. Like most of the houses on the curving street, there was a three-car garage, a postage-stamp lawn and a wide entry.

In this case, there was also a woman on the porch wrestling with an oversize, metal-framed screen door.

Logan smiled to himself as he got out of the car. Janice was no shy, retiring female, but he hadn't pictured her as a handyman, either. She did, however, look fit in a pair of shorts and a tank top, her skin a golden tan.

At mid afternoon, the late-August sun baked down on the neighborhood, drying out the lawns and softening the tar strip between the asphalt of the street and the concrete gutter. He walked up the driveway and onto the walkway to the house just as Janice swore under her breath.

"Could you use some help?" he asked mildly.

She whirled, still balancing the screen door with her shoulder. Both her smile and her surprise were genuine. "Logan! Oh, my gosh! I didn't hear you drive up."

Firefighters and their families socialized frequently, although Janice wasn't always part of the group. Logan was secretly pleased at her instant recognition and her warm smile.

He reached for the pre-fab screen door, which included hinges and a latch, and held it up. "Looks like you were otherwise occupied."

"Tell me about it." Using her forearm, she swiped at the sweat on her forehead. Her dark hair glistened with the same perspiration, the natural curl frizzing around her face in a sable outline that emphasized its heart shape. "I've been telling Ray for years we needed a screen door to let the west breeze in on hot days and to keep out the flies. He finally bought the door a year ago but he never—" She stopped abruptly, then shrugged. "I decided if I was going to get my screen door, I'd have to do it myself."

Logan pulled the door away from her. It was fairly heavy since the bottom half was ionized metal, only the top half a screen. "I'll do it."

She studied him a moment, her ginger-brown eyes assessing him. He saw lines of fatigue around her eyes, a sense of being overwhelmed in their depths, and none of the sparkle that had drawn him in during their prior encounters, despite her marital status. The urge to restore her optimistic spirit rose with the speed of a flame racing up a gasoline-drenched wall, and he forced himself to remember she'd been recently widowed. And why.

Slowly, she shook her head. "I'm trying to learn to stand on my own two feet."

"Great. Think of me as a hired hand. My price is a cool glass of lemonade or a beer, whatever you've got."

Relinquishing her hold on the door, she stepped back. "I really hate it that I don't know how to do certain chores around the house. Ray always said he'd take care of things, forget my honey-do list was about two miles long. He didn't like the idea of me doing a man's job."

"So let me get this door installed and you can check off one of the honey-do's."

"Guess I shouldn't look a gift horse in the mouth."

"That's what friends are for." Resting the screen against the doorjamb, Logan examined the contents of the tool caddie on the porch. It looked as if Ray had amassed everything he needed. "Have you got the screws?"

"Oh, yes." Janice pulled a packet of screws from her back pocket and handed it to Logan. He was a quiet, serious man, one of her favorite people to talk with at firefighter get-togethers. A gentle spirit in a powerful body, she'd always thought.

Today he was wearing faded beige Dockers and a cotton sport shirt that tugged across his wide shoulders and tucked in at a narrow waist. His sandy-brown hair was trimmed to a medium length and combed back, lying neatly on his well-shaped head. Unlike some of the firefighters Janice knew, Logan always looked pulled together, even on his days off.

She'd often wondered why such a tall, good-looking firefighter wasn't married, but she'd never thought it was her business to ask. Certainly Ray wouldn't have been pleased if she'd expressed any particular interest in another man.

She watched as Logan measured where the hinges would go and marked the screw holes with a pencil. He appeared comfortable in the role of carpenter, going about the task with a minimum of wasted effort. She'd always thought of him as unflappable, both personally and on the job. A good firefighter.

"So how's it going?" he asked as he picked up a drill and slid in a bit, tightening it in place.

"Some days are better than others." The first week after Ray's death had been a total blur, her children distraught, relatives coming in from out of town, neighbors helping out, firefighters and their wives trying to lend a hand.

She still felt numb, not so much with grief, although that was part of it, but with the frightening array of decisions she'd had to make. Ray hadn't been real good about keeping her in the loop.

"My biggest problem right now is getting the insurance money. Chief Gray says the state is always slow. Since Ray was only in the department six years, what little pension I get barely covers the grocery bill."

Lowering the drill, Logan looked at her, his gaze both sympathetic and intense. His eyes were hazel with touches of green and gold, she mused, realizing this was the first time she'd noticed that detail.

"There's a widows' and orphans' fund that can help out in an emergency."

"We'll be all right. I filed the papers a couple of weeks ago for the life insurance we've been paying for since Kevin was born. I had to wait for copies of the, ah—" she stumbled over the word and swallowed hard, still unable to totally accept the fact that Ray was dead "—death certificate before I could do that."

To her amazement, he tenderly cupped her face with his hand, using his thumb to wipe away a tear she hadn't known she'd shed. His gentleness nearly undid her. She was striving so hard to survive on her own, she didn't dare let herself fall apart. She might never be able to pull herself together again.

"I'm sorry," she murmured, a lump of determination lodging in her throat. "I didn't use to spring leaks like that at the drop of a hat."

"You were very brave at the funeral. Ray would have been proud of you."

"You think so?"

"Yeah. I know I thought you were pretty terrific. The kids, too."

She closed her hand around his wrist, holding on for a moment as though she could draw from his inner strength. "If I never hear bagpipes playing a funeral dirge again, it'll be just fine with me."

One side of his mouth lifted in a wry smile. "Someday I'll play a Scottish jig for you on the pipes. That will lift your spirits."

"You play that awful, squealing instrument?" she gasped.

He laughed out loud, a deep baritone that rumbled through his chest. "In my family, criticizing pipe playing is sacrilegious. My brother Derek and I are fourth-generation firefighters and about tenth-generation pipers. But I admit it's probably an acquired taste."

"I'll agree with that." She found herself smiling back at him, her first real smile in, well, a month. Having Logan around was like a dose of chin-up medicine. "I'll go stir up some lemonade. The kids are down the block swimming in a neighbor's pool, but they'll be back soon and probably ready for something cool to drink."

"Then I'd better get busy so I can earn my keep."

Logan waited until she'd gone into the house, then slowly exhaled. What the hell had made him touch her? Her skin was so damn soft, so warm. He'd known it would be, which is why he shouldn't have come within arm's reach of Janice, the widow of a man whose life he might have saved if he'd acted more wisely.

His hand shook as he lifted the drill and drove the bit into the doorjamb. Wood shavings curled back around the quarter-inch hole. Thank goodness his pants were loose enough that the telltale bulge behind his zipper hadn't been obvious. Talk about lousy timing. He didn't dare let his feelings for Janice get out of hand. Right now, what she needed was a friend, not some lust-crazed firefighter with an overactive libido.

Within minutes, Janice reappeared, carrying a tray with a pitcher of lemonade and four plastic cups.

"My gracious! You've already got the door hung."

He opened the door for her so she could carry the tray outside. "It wasn't that hard. I've still got to hook up the spring, though, so the door will close by itself, and then install the latch plate."

"You're a miracle worker, Logan. That door's been gathering dust in the garage ever since I coerced Ray into buying it."

"Half the battle is getting started on a project. The rest is easy."

Setting the tray on the top step, she poured a glass of lemonade and handed it to Logan. Ice cubes rattled as he took a big swallow.

"In Ray's defense, he was working awfully hard on his second job. It took most of his free time, but he wanted to build up our nest egg for the kids' college money. You know how expensive an education can be these days."

Logan's eyebrows lifted. "His second job?"

"You know, the sales thing he was doing. He had to do a lot of travelling."

That was news to Logan. Except that…on the morning of the fatal fire, Ray had arrived at the station late, not for the first time in recent memory. He'd been hungover and had complained about lack of sleep plus a long drive from Las Vegas back to Paseo. Grousing around, he'd been in no shape to fight a wastebasket fire, much less a three-alarm blaze in an abandoned warehouse.

"I don't think Ray mentioned his job to me," Logan admitted. "He probably told the other guys, though."

She poured herself some lemonade. "I don't know. You fellows seem to spend all your time talking about your heroic deeds with a fire hose, like you're trying to impress each other."

"It's called one up-manship. An old tradition among firefighters."

"It goes along with playing bagpipes, I assume."

"Only a guy who's really tough can get away with wearing a kilt."

Her smile reached her eyes, making them glisten with good humor. "You gotta be tough *and* have great legs."

"I have it on good authority my knees are knobby."

Her gaze skimmed down his legs, and to his amazement, Logan felt the heat of a blush creep up his neck.

"I don't think so," she said softly. "It seems to me at department picnics, the wives have rated your legs right up there with the best of 'em."

"Terrific," he groaned as the heat reached his cheeks. "I always wondered what you women were giggling about when we men were giving it our all on the baseball diamond."

"Now you know."

He already knew more than he wanted to—that Janice had a great sense of humor and that he was more attracted to her than he cared to admit, even to himself. While she was married, he hadn't had any trouble keeping his distance. He ought to feel the same way about a newly widowed woman—she was off limits. But he was having trouble remembering that.

Fortunately, the arrival of the mail carrier saved him from making a fool of himself.

"Afternoon, Ms. Gainer. Another load of junk mail for your recycling pile." The young black woman, wearing navy-blue uniform shorts and a light blue shirt, handed over a thick fold of mail. "Hope you all are doing okay these days."

"We're fine, Alice. Thanks for asking."

"I've been praying for you and your children. Your husband was a hero, Ms. Gainer. The whole town says so. It's an honor to know you."

Nodding, Janice looked embarrassed by the young woman's praise. She glanced down and began to sort through the mail as the carrier went striding back down the walkway.

"You okay?" Logan asked.

She shrugged. "Sometimes it's hardest when people...she meant well enough, but a dead hero isn't what I had in mind for a husband."

Logan understood that. Worse, he was the one person who knew Ray hadn't been a hero that day. He'd been an arrogant, hard-headed fool who hadn't listened to Logan's warning that the roof was about to collapse.

She lifted an envelope from the pile and ripped it open. "At last, the insurance company. This has got to be the check." Unfolding a white sheet of stationery, she read it over, then sat down heavily on the top step of the porch. "This can't be right," she murmured. The color had fled her cheeks, and her trembling hand caused the letter to flutter. "It can't be."

Logan squatted down beside her. "What is it?"

"They say—" she shook her head "—they're claiming the insurance policy lapsed more than a year ago because of lack of payment. But Ray—" She looked up at Logan with disbelief in her eyes. "Ray knew how important that money would be if something happened to him. I was supposed to pay off the mortgage with it. The children, me, that was our protection. Then the death benefit from the state would see us through for several years, till I could get a decent job. We'd talked about it. He *knew* we'd need the house paid off."

Logan slipped the letter from her hand and read it quickly. "Maybe it's a mistake. If you can find the canceled check, they'll have to pay you the benefits. This is a reputable company. They'll meet their obligations."

"But what if Ray didn't make the payments? What if he forgot? What will I do?" Her expression shifted, disbelief replaced by fear, deepening her eyes to a dark brown and sheening them with tears. "What in heaven's name will I do? I've already got bills to pay. The funeral home. The fee for the plot. Dear God—"

"You're not going to panic, that's the first thing." He rested his hand on her shoulder, stroking lightly. The funeral service had been huge, with every member of Paseo del Real's fire department present while neighboring towns had covered in case an emergency occurred. Representatives from half the fire departments in the state and many from across the country had shown up. Police had been out in full force, so had many members of the community. Through it all, Janice had been a chin-up trouper. Her kids, too, considering their ages. Now she was falling apart. Logan was glad he was here to catch some of the pieces. "Then you're going to go through your bank records. Chances are good you'll find this is all a mistake. Meanwhile, the emergency fund will tide you over with whatever you and the kids need in order to get by."

Her body shuddered beneath his hand. Vulnerable. Needing support. He tried not to think about how much he'd like to be the one she needed. Knowing what he did, he couldn't be that man. Not for the long haul.

"I've been trying to sort through the records, but it's like a maze. He had a half-dozen checking accounts. Some of them are closed, the others don't show any balance at all. And I had no idea how many credit cards we had. It's as though someone was handing them out like candy, and Ray accepted every offer that came his way."

"Look, I don't mean to butt in, but if you want me to, I'll help you check through the records. Maybe together we can straighten this out." Although he had the niggling feeling that whatever they found out wouldn't be good news for Janice. Closed accounts and too many credit cards were a bad sign.

"I've been such a fool." Her voice caught. "On all those talk shows, they warn you that a wife ought to know what's going on financially. But Ray didn't—" She fingered a grocery store flyer that had been delivered with the letter. "He didn't think I was the smartest fish in the pond. He said he'd take care of everything."

Resisting the urge to bunch his hands into fists, Logan wrapped his arm around her. Her hair smelled of a floral scent, like wild blossoms on a spring hillside. Fresh and invigorating. Elemental. So feminine it made him ache for her.

Damn it! She deserved better than to have been kept in the dark about the family finances. She deserved more than to be told she was dumb. She deserved somebody who would value her as the incredible woman that she was.

"Don't throw in the towel yet, Jan. There's still the state benefits, and the city provides something."

She inhaled a shuddering breath. "I know. It's just that—"

From across the street, two children came running, Janice's son Kevin in the lead with five-year-old Maddie bringing up the rear.

"What are you doing to my mom?" Kevin demanded.

Janice broke away from Logan as though she'd been goosed. "Kevin, you remember Logan Strong, he rode on the ladder truck with your father."

Kevin glared at Logan as if he'd committed some mortal sin—something that wasn't ever going to happen, Logan reminded himself. At least not between him and Janice.

"Hey, Kevin," he said. "How's it going?"

The nine-year-old eyed him suspiciously. "My dad was a hero."

"Yep," Logan agreed. "That's what they say."

The chip on the boy's shoulder was about ten feet high. "I'm gonna be a hero, too."

"Good for you, son. I'm sure—"

"I'm not your son!"

Properly chastised, Logan agreed. "You're right. But if you were, I'd be darn proud of you."

The boy did a double take. "You would?"

"Sure. You take care of your mom, and your little sister, too. That's pretty impressive for a nine-year-old kid."

The youngster lifted his shoulders in a shrug that wasn't all that uncaring. "I'll do better when I'm grown up."

Logan suppressed a smile. "I'm sure you will."

Arriving at full speed, Maddie lunged into her mother's lap. "Kevin cheated. He got a head start on me."

Automatically, Janice stroked her daughter's crop of dark, flyaway hair. "Look what Mr. Strong did for us. He hung the screen door."

"My dad was gonna do that." Curious, Kevin opened the screen. "He's real good at stuff like this."

"He had some nice tools," Logan said. "The door still needs a spring and a latch. You could help me with the rest of the job."

The boy glanced at his mother for guidance.

Maddie popped to her feet. "I'll help you."

Before Logan could respond, Janice said, "If you

let these two minxes help, it'll be another year before the job's finished."

"It shouldn't take too long. We just have to install a screw eye, fix the latch plate and we'll be all set."

Janice looked at him skeptically. "You haven't been around children much, have you?"

"I've got a couple of nephews but they live in Merced."

"Well..." Smiling, she rose to her feet, the mail still in her hand. "Don't say I didn't warn you."

Two hours later, Logan discovered he should have listened to Janice's warning. The kids had argued over every step, little sister insisting she was big enough to use a drill, big brother insisting she wasn't, and Logan scared one or the other of them would ram the drill right through his palm while he was guiding their small hands. That didn't begin to cover his concerns about them using a chisel and hammer.

Finally he sent them both into the house to announce that the job was finished, and he put the tools away.

Janice appeared on the other side of the screen door. She'd changed into a clean pair of shorts and it looked like she'd done something with her hair, the natural curl softer now. More touchable.

"You must have the patience of a saint."

"If I do, it's the only thing saintly about me." Certainly his thoughts were anything but holy when it came to Janice.

"We're having tacos and refried beans for dinner.

It's not much in the way of a thank-you, but will you stay?''

"I probably ought to get going," he hedged.

"I was hoping after dinner, when the kids are in bed and we can get a little quiet around here, you'd help me make sense of Ray's record-keeping. But if you have something to do—''

"No. Nothing important." He only had an empty house to go home to, no one waiting for him on the porch that overlooked the small fishing lake in the foothills of the coastal range, an hour's drive from Paseo del Real. His hideaway, his family called it. That wasn't far from the truth.

JANICE COULD BARELY remember the last time she'd served a man his dinner. Not that tacos and beans at the kitchen table qualified as anything special. But with Ray's shift work, and then his second job, he'd been little more than a shadow member of the family, the most obvious sign he'd been home a new heap of dirty clothes in the hamper.

How long had she been living like that, more housekeeper than wife? And why, she wondered with a pang of guilt, was her grief colored with an edge of relief that Ray was gone?

Setting aside her troubling thoughts, she served up four plates and carried them to the table.

"You want that beer now?" she asked.

"I'll have a beer," Kevin piped up.

She punched him affectionately on his shoulder. "Milk or lemonade, big guy?"

"Lemonade," he conceded.

"Lemonade is fine by me, too," Logan assured her, winking at her son.

Kevin started eating right away, but Janice noticed Logan waited until she was seated and had picked up her fork. She'd let Kevin's manners slip recently. Without Ray around, it had been easier to let things slide.

Her throat tightened, and she laid her fork down. Whatever chance they might have had to get their marriage back on track was gone now. Forever.

"You okay?" Logan asked from across the table.

Lifting her head, she met his gaze. He had the most sympathetic eyes, a penetrating way of looking at her as though he understood her pain. Her loneliness.

The guilt that she hadn't been a better wife. Regret that she couldn't mourn as deeply as others expected her to.

"I'm fine." She forked some beans into her mouth and forced herself to swallow. "Ray used to rave about your clam linguini and said you were the best cook on C-shift. I guess tacos are pretty simple fare—"

"They're perfect. Just what a man needs after hanging a screen door. Isn't that right, Kevin?"

The boy looked up, startled. "Yeah. Mom's tacos are the best."

With a smile, Janice basked in her son's compliment. Oddly, she felt like a houseplant that had been denied water for too long and at last someone had noticed. She drank in the refreshing nourishment Logan had made possible along with his praise. Then she felt foolish for making such a big deal out of something so insignificant.

"I help my mommy make cookies sometimes," Maddie said around a mouth full of taco.

"I bet you're good at it, too," Logan responded.

Kevin scraped the last of his beans from his plate. "Chief Gray gave Dad a Medal of Honor postumlous."

"Posthumously," Janice supplied.

"Anyway, you wanna see it? Mom lets me keep it in my room but I can't take it to school 'cause I might lose it. I've got the flag they put over his casket, too. They told me it used to fly at the White House where the president lives."

"Logan may not be—"

"Sure, I'd like to see it. After we finish dinner, okay?"

Kevin beamed his pleasure, and Janice's heart squeezed tight. Her son needed a man to show interest in him. Since Ray's death, the boy had been more angry than sad. In a few short hours, Logan had turned Kevin's sullen expression into one of anticipation. He'd make a wonderful father.

Janice started at that thought. Ray had been gone only a month and she was already betraying him by comparing her husband to another man. She couldn't do that.

Ray's children needed to honor their father's memory. She needed to help them do that by being loyal to his memory, too.

Acknowledging her attraction to another man, even to herself, would risk undermining the needs of her children. For Janice, her children had to come first. Not a fanciful relationship with a gentle giant who was only trying to be kind to her.

Chapter Two

Glancing around the cluttered office, Logan shook his head. After the kids had finally gone to bed, he and Janice had spent several hours going through financial records.

"I've got to say, Ray wasn't the most organized man I've ever seen," Logan commented, in what had to be the world's biggest understatement.

Janice sat cross-legged in the middle of the room, the picture of dejection. Checkbooks and bank statements surrounded her, credit-card reports piled at her side.

She sighed. "This is bad, isn't it?"

Logan hunkered down beside her, wishing he could find something encouraging to say. "We sure haven't found any sign Ray paid the insurance premium in the past couple of years."

"If we were in such terrible financial trouble that we couldn't afford it, why didn't he tell me?"

"I don't know."

"For that matter, how did it happen? I mean, when we bought the house it was well within our budget.

I've hardly been extravagant with my spending, and except for Ray's convertible, neither was he.''

While sifting through the credit-card statements, Logan had noted Ray was only paying the minimum amount each month, which meant the interest was building up. And there were a hell of a lot of charges from Las Vegas—hotels, restaurants, expensive items. Some pretty fancy meals locally, too. None of the charges looked like the bills any salesman Logan knew would run up.

An uneasy feeling crept up his spine. He was damn curious about Ray's *sales* job, assuming he actually had been moonlighting and not indulging in activities a wife wouldn't want to hear about. Ray had been closed-mouthed, kind of standoffish. He hadn't socialized much with the guys on their days off, which Logan had taken to mean he was busy with his family. Now he wasn't so sure. He sure as hell hadn't heard a hint about Ray holding down a second job.

Dropping her head into her hands, Janice groaned, ''What am I going to do?''

''Shh, it's going to be okay.'' Tentatively, Logan stroked her hair in a gesture much like she'd used with her daughter, except he wasn't feeling at all parental. Her husband might have screwed up, but Logan was sure the state benefits would tide her over, at least for the near term. ''I want you to come down to the station tomorrow and talk to Chief Gray. He's a good man and cares about his troops. He'll make sure you get what's coming to you.''

She lifted her chin and looked him in the eye. ''I

didn't want to ask for extra help. Ray wouldn't have wanted me to—''

"Ray would want you and the kids to be taken care of.''

"Then why did he forget to pay—''

"I don't know, Jan." He had the troubling feeling there was more to her husband's neglect than met the eye. "At this point, it doesn't matter. What you need to do is deal with one problem at a time. Paying the bills is the first problem. We'll deal with the rest later.''

Gathering herself, she leaned back against the desk leg and wrapped her arms around her midsection. "Why aren't you married?"

Her question caught him off guard. He didn't often mention that part of his past. "I was. Briefly. It got so that my wife hated the sound of a siren. She couldn't stand the thought of the fire chief pulling up in our driveway in his red car to announce I'd been killed in a fire. I guess you can understand that.''

Visibly, Janice shuddered. "A firefighter's wife's worst nightmare. I knew when I saw Chief Gray—'' She glanced away. The pain was so visible on her face, in her every gesture, Logan knew she'd never put herself at risk like that again. Or her children.

He didn't blame her. Despite the fact his mother and his sister-in-law managed to survive knowing that any given day could be their husband's last, he understood why his wife hadn't been able to handle that reality. And he hadn't been willing to give up the career that was a family tradition.

Since then, he'd vowed never to subject another woman to the same possibility. Certainly not a woman who'd already lost one husband to the job. That would be the worst form of cruelty.

Janice scooped up the bank statements and stacked them neatly. "Someone very wise once said there was no sense crying over spilled milk. The kids and I sure could have used that insurance money, but if this is the worst that happens as a result of Ray's death, we'll get by."

"I think my mother used to say things like that."

"Mine, too. My dad just yelled at us kids whether we spilled anything or not." She smiled at him and started to get up.

Instinctively Logan reached for her elbow. "You've got brothers and sisters?"

"Three brothers and two sisters, all of them in Missouri. That's where I met Ray, while he was in the air force. He convinced me to drop out of college and come west with him. Truth to tell, it didn't take much urging. I couldn't see much of a future for myself in the small town where I grew up."

"And I suppose you were in love."

Frowning, she picked up some more papers, sorted them and put them in a manila folder. "A man in uniform is hard for a girl to resist."

Logan noted her hesitation, the odd way she'd phrased her response, and wondered about it. Not that Janice's relationship with her husband was any of his business. His role was that of a concerned friend. Nothing more.

He glanced at his watch, suddenly realizing the hour had grown late. "Guess I'd better get going. I'm on duty tomorrow."

She walked him toward the front of the house. "Thanks for hanging the screen door. I can't tell you how many years I've wanted one of those."

"No problem. Let me know if there are any other chores you need doing. I'm pretty handy with a screwdriver."

"Well, there is that ten-page list in the kitchen that I was telling you about, if you're really interested."

He laughed. "I'll drop by next week and see what I can do. Meanwhile, thanks for dinner."

"You're more than welcome. I really do appreciate your help." She extended her hand.

For a heartbeat, Logan hesitated, then took her hand in his. Her skin was too soft to wield a hammer, her fingers too delicate to twist a screwdriver. Instead, her hand was made for caressing a man's flesh, soothing him after a long day. Arousing him.

Abruptly releasing her hand, he cleared his throat. "You'll come by to talk to the chief tomorrow?"

"Yes." She gazed into his eyes as though she had felt the same frisson of sexual awareness. "I'm determined to get my life together and not depend on anyone else, but I can't let my pride stand in the way of taking care of my children. For now, I'll have to ask for help."

"There's no sin in that, Janice. You'll always be a part of the firefighter family, and we take care of our own."

It was just a damn shame he felt something a lot more potent than brotherly affection for her.

JANICE PARKED her minivan behind Station Six in the employee lot, and the kids scrambled out. The main fire station in Paseo del Real stood three stories tall with living quarters on the top two floors and administrative offices at street level. The open bay of the main building housed two fire engines, a paramedic unit and the ladder truck her husband used to ride. A training tower occupied the far corner of the property.

Before she could warn Kevin not to, he hopped on the heavy wrought-iron gate that led to a back patio area and swung it for all he was worth. If she hadn't known better, Janice would have sworn her son was part monkey. He'd swing from anything that held still long enough for him to climb on. To his father's dismay, more times than not.

"I wanna swing, too," Maddie complained.

"You're too little," Kevin countered.

"Uh-uh!" The five-year-old grabbed onto one of the bars, only to discover she had to run to keep up with her brother.

"Whoa, you two!" Janice snared Maddie's arm before the child took a tumble. "Let's try not to break our necks, okay? I've got to see Chief Gray, and I'd just as soon you two stayed in one piece till I do." Under the circumstances, she'd also prefer not to run up any medical bills because her children were overly energetic.

"But Mommy—" Maddie whined.

Fortunately Buttons, a chocolate dalmatian who was the station mascot, arrived to save the day.

"Buttons!" Forgetting all about swinging on the gate with her brother, Maddie raced to greet her canine buddy. The dog lapped at her face with his long tongue, and she giggled.

Her heart squeezing on a rush of love, Janice smiled at her daughter. Ray had never wanted the children to have a dog or even a cat. He'd claimed a pet would be too much work for him, although it was clear Janice would have carried most of the responsibility for an animal. Maybe now that he was gone—

She abruptly halted the thought as a guilty sense of betrayal washed over her. She shouldn't be thinking about the good things that might happen because Ray had died a heroic death. Right now, she simply needed to concentrate on the survival of her family.

Hank Smyth, the engineer who drove the ladder truck, waved at her from across the way. "Hey, Janice, how's it going?"

She waved back. "One day at a time."

A moment later, another firefighter had come out to greet her. And then another. Before long, she was surrounded by well-wishers. As Logan had said, firefighters were a family and they hadn't disowned her yet.

"Look," she said, "I've got to go talk to the chief."

"We'll watch the kids," Hank volunteered.

"I'm in charge of Maddie," Greg Turrick announced, swooping the child into the air and making her scream in delight. As was his custom, he burst into a country-western song about her being the love of his life, which turned Maddie's screams into giggles.

"You got 'em, gentlemen. But be careful. They're my life now."

The smiles she got in return let Janice know the men were grieving, too, and doing what they could for her.

Blinking away a fresh crop of tears, she turned toward the entrance to the offices. Damn it! If she didn't stop "leaking" soon, she'd have to start taping tissues to her cheeks.

She'd barely started down the hallway to the chief's office when Emma Jean Witkowsky stepped out of the door marked Dispatch. The jingle of silver bracelets accompanied her steps, her dark hair bouncing in rhythm.

"Oh, Janice, honey, I'm so glad to see you." Emma Jean gave her a quick hug. "I've been reading my crystal ball and the news is wonderful. Absolutely wonderful!"

"Is that anything like a network bulletin interrupting regular programming?" In spite of her troubles, Janice couldn't help teasing the fire station's resident gypsy-psychic who, according to informed sources, got more of her predictions wrong than right.

"No, of course not." Emma Jean laughed. "It's just that your future looks rosy." She frowned. "Of course, it's a new ball I'm using, and I've only been taking crystal-ball-reading classes for a couple of months. It's a correspondence course. So, to make sure everything's going to be okay, maybe I ought to read your palm—''

Janice brushed a kiss to Emma Jean's cheek. "I'm sure my future is in good hands. Thanks for caring." It was the next couple of months Janice was worried about, not the long-term future. She had to believe that somehow everything would work out. A crystal ball wouldn't help her. She'd have to do it herself.

A few steps down the hallway, she discovered Logan waiting for her outside the chief's door. In his dark-blue uniform with its sharply creased pants and wrinkle-free shirt, he looked stunning, a perfect model for *Firefighters Monthly*. She swallowed hard at the thought.

"I heard you were here," he said in a low, intimate voice. "You look nice."

A flush crept up her neck. She'd worn a simple skirt, a summery blouse and sandals. It wasn't exactly a professional outfit—and certainly not suitable if someone had expected to see her in deep mourning—but she'd wanted to make an upbeat impression on Chief Gray. Which was silly, since he already knew her. Still, she was inordinately pleased with Logan's compliment.

"You look pretty good yourself, fireman," she teased.

"They tell me I clean up okay."

Amen to that. Logan Strong always drew one of the top bids at the annual Bachelor Auction to benefit the burn unit at the local hospital. If he weren't such a kind, sympathetic man who obviously felt some responsibility to help the widow of a man he'd worked with, Janice wouldn't be spending much time with Logan. She'd simply be grateful for whatever help he offered. Beyond that, she'd have to keep her imagination in check.

No way had he felt the same sense of intimacy, of forbidden sexual excitement, that she had last night when they'd said goodbye. To even consider that possibility was to deceive herself.

Hadn't Ray made it clear she wasn't the hottest thing between the covers? There was no reason to suspect Logan would ever be attracted to her.

Besides, her loyalty belonged to her husband. It was far too soon even to be considering a relationship with any other man.

"The chief's waiting," Logan said when she didn't speak. "I just wanted to say hello and wish you luck."

"Thanks," she mumbled.

"If you're still here at lunch, there's plenty for you and the kids. You could stick around."

"Kevin and Maddie would like that." Both children had idolized their father and his career, the few visits they'd made to the fire station highlights in their young lives. Janice wouldn't deny them that joy now that their father was gone.

LEAVING JANICE at the chief's office, Logan walked upstairs and sat down alone at one end of the picnic-style dining table. The crew of Engine 61 had kitchen duty. Usually, a couple of times a week, whoever was stuck with the cooking would pay Logan a little extra to handle the task—pocket change. But not today. For the past month he'd turned down all their offers. Since the warehouse fire that had killed Ray, his heart hadn't been in eating, much less cooking.

Or much of anything else, he realized. Unable to look them in the eye, he'd kept his distance from his fellow firefighters. In his own mind, he deserved to be ostracized from the brotherhood for not having taken the steps that would have saved Ray's life.

Even during physical training this morning when the men of Station Six had jogged around a six-mile course at the local park and then done calisthenics, he'd lingered at the back of the pack. Keeping his distance. Acting like an arsonist afraid of being caught.

The same thing would happen this afternoon when they had a white-board training session on handling hazardous materials scheduled. Even if there were empty chairs, he'd stand at the back of the room.

Because if he got too close to these men who knew him so well, they'd see the truth about what had happened that morning. Logan would be the one to destroy the memory of a firefighter and make the medal his son showed off so proudly no more meaningful than a piece of scrap metal.

He couldn't do that. In the brotherhood of firefighters, loyalty demanded that he keep his mouth shut and his damning knowledge to himself.

Over the loudspeaker, Mike Gables announced lunch was ready and men began to wander into the dining area for a menu of make-your-own sandwiches, apples, cookies and potato chips. Pretty simple fare.

Logan decided he'd wait for Janice and her children.

Getting up from the table, he wandered to the window overlooking the back of the station. Maddie was playing chase-the-dog's-tail with Buttons; Kevin was hanging out with Tommy Tonka on Big Red, the 1930s-vintage fire engine the teenager was helping firefighters to restore. If all went well, the shiny rebuilt engine would lead the Founder's Day parade in the fall. That was assuming they could find a new transmission or remake the old one.

He smiled as he saw Janice come out of the station. A breeze caught her skirt, molding it against her slender legs as she said something to her kids. A moment later, they all headed back inside. They'd be coming upstairs soon.

Silently he acknowledged he'd been unduly impatient to see her today. She might not be beautiful in the classic sense, but her genuine smile and the way her light-brown eyes lit up when she laughed had always tugged at something elemental within him. A reaction he needed to continue suppressing.

He met Janice and the kids at the top of the stairs.

''We get to eat lunch here with the firemens,'' Maddie announced, as excited as most youngsters would be about a trip to McDonalds.

With mock formality, he bowed them into the dining room. ''Step right up to the counter, ladies and gentlemen. All the ham and cheese sandwiches you can eat.''

Maddie giggled, Kevin swaggered ahead of his sister and Janice bestowed one of her heart-stopping smiles on Logan. He tried to remember she smiled at everyone that way and simply be glad he'd done something to boost her spirits.

Helping the trio get their lunches organized, Logan served himself last, then sat down at a table opposite Janice.

"How'd it go with the chief?" he asked.

"He'll get me a check within two days, so the monkey is off my back for the moment."

"Are we getting a monkey, Mommy?" Maddie asked around a mouthful of sandwich, mustard creasing the corners of her lips.

"No, honey. That's just an expression."

"Can we get a dog instead? One just like Buttons? I love him *soooo* much."

From down the table, Mike Gables said, "My son's dog Suzie is expecting, and we think Buttons could be the daddy. We're looking for good homes for the—"

With a laugh, Janice held up her hand to halt Mike's offer. "Why don't we wait on that for a while?"

Formerly the most studly bachelor in the Paseo del Real fire department, Mike had recently married and settled into family life with an adopted six-year-old son and the boy's former social worker. The youngster's ragamuffin dog had been part of the package, a shaggy female of indiscriminate breed. Questionable morals, too, Logan thought with a grin.

"But Mommy, I'd *love* Buttons' babies to *pieces*."

"Yes, dear, I know." Janice smoothed her hand

over her daughter's hair. "Eat your lunch now, honey. We'll talk about getting a dog later."

Kevin shoved his empty plate aside. "I'm all done, Mom. Can I go down the fire pole now?"

"You certainly may *not!* You know your father never allowed you to do that."

"But, gee—"

Logan swallowed a chuckle. The pole that firefighters slid down to the fire engines when an alarm sounded was like a magnet to kids. During school field trips, a man was stationed at the doorway to make sure a youngster didn't take an unauthorized ride down the pole—or inadvertently fall into the three-story-deep hole that surrounded it. But the children of firefighters generally sneaked a slide at least once as they were growing up. Kevin was plenty old enough to give it a try—but not when his mother was telling him no.

Coaxing Maddie to take a couple more bites of sandwich, Janice finished her own meal, then announced it was time for her to go. "I've got to take the children shopping for shoes. School starts next week."

"I'm going to be in kenner-garden," Maddie said proudly.

Logan smiled at her. "I bet you'll be the smartest kid in the class, too."

"I already know my letters and I can write my own name."

"Good for you, sprite." Collecting the empty plates before Janice could, Logan said, "Hang on a sec while I dump the trash. I'll walk you downstairs."

She waited, although the children didn't. Kevin,

wearing thick-soled, designer running shoes, the laces untied, thundered down the stairs with Maddie fast on his heels.

Janice followed more sedately, her hips moving with a natural grace. "I don't know how my mother survived raising six kids. Those two wear me out."

"You're doing fine. They're great kids."

At the first-floor landing, she turned to look up at him. "Actually, my mother once told me that after three children, it becomes a crowd and they all entertain each other. I thought of us kids as a mob scene, but we did have some good times together."

"Did you want more children?" Before the words were out, Logan knew he should have bitten his tongue. "I'm sorry. Under the circumstances, that was a really thoughtless question."

"No, it wasn't." She shrugged. "I did want more children. Being a mother is one of the few things I do really well. But Ray wasn't all that happy about Kevin—we hadn't been married long—and then when I got pregnant with Maddie..." She let the thought dangle.

Logan frowned at that. He'd like to have kids of his own, but without a wife that wasn't likely to happen, and he couldn't imagine a man not being thrilled by any child that was his. "I'd say if Maddie hadn't come along, then both you and Ray would have missed out on something special."

Her wistful smile nearly undid him. "I know," she said softly. "I told him that the day Maddie was born."

As they stepped through the doorway into the bay area, her gaze scanned past the parked fire engine to spot her children. Kevin was back to the restored fire truck, turning it into a jungle gym. Maddie was nowhere in sight.

"Maddie!" Janice called. "It's time to go."

"Maybe she's already out at your car," Logan suggested.

"More likely she's discussing puppies with Buttons." She cupped her hands and shouted for Maddie again.

This time the child appeared from around the back of the fire station, Buttons faithfully at her side. The guilty look on the little girl's face was as obvious as if someone had painted a big letter G on her forehead.

"What have you been up to?" her mother asked.

Maddie hung her head. "Nuthin'."

"And what are you hiding behind your back?"

Slowly, the child extended her hand. "A pencil."

Logan stepped forward to retrieve the item. It wasn't a pencil but rather a thick purple felt pen like the ones the department used for white-board sessions. Harmless, he thought, until he examined Buttons more closely.

"Janice, I think you'd better come take a look at this."

Cocking her head to the side, she scrutinized Buttons. "Oh, Maddie, what have you done?"

The child puffed out her lower lip. "I liked Buttons' spots and I thought he'd look nice with more spots."

"*Purple* spots?" Janice choked out, barely able to contain her laughter.

Logan was in the same fix. His stomach muscles ached from holding back a howl of his own.

The fire tone shattered the lighthearted moment. Over the loudspeaker the distorted voice of Emma Jean, the dispatcher, announced, "Engines 61 and 62, Ladder 67. Structure fire, Broadway and Twenty-fifth—"

Before the directions were finished, Logan had turned away. But the quick touch of Janice's hand on his arm, as soft as a butterfly landing, halted him. He glanced back, seeing the echo of fear in her soft, brown eyes.

"Be careful," she whispered.

He nodded. "I always am."

Turning again, he raced to the ladder truck, stepping into his heavy, fire-resistant bunker pants that he'd earlier stacked on the floor beside the truck, and he slipped his feet into his boots. He pulled his suspenders up in one fluid motion before reaching for his heavy turnout jacket. At the same time, he swung into the backward-facing seat where his helmet was waiting. The truck vibrated as the engineer started the motor and the smell of exhaust fumes filled the bay.

Seconds later, they were speeding out of the fire station behind the two fire engines, heading north on Paseo Boulevard, sirens screaming.

Logan kept his eyes on Janice's stricken face until the truck rounded the corner.

The vow he'd made never to make a woman dread the sound of a siren was a good one.

Still, he couldn't help wishing someday a woman like Janice Gainer would be waiting for him when he got off a shift, to rejoice in his safe return.

Chapter Three

The second day of school and already Janice missed her children. It had been bad enough when Kevin had gone off to kindergarten, but then she'd had Maddie to keep her company. Now the silent house mocked the maternal trauma of sending her youngest child to school.

They were both growing up so fast.

She went into the laundry room to take the clothes out of the dryer only to discover the barricade of towels she'd arranged around the bottom of the washing machine had sprung a leak. A puddle of water spread out across the vinyl no-wax floor.

"Oh, damn," she muttered. Ray was supposed to have fixed the plumbing months ago. She couldn't go on indefinitely trying to mop up the mess. Eventually the flooring underneath would get wet and rot. She'd have to call a plumber.

The doorbell rang, and she rolled her eyes. Who on earth—

In a peevish mood, she marched to the front of the house, peered through the peep hole in the door, and suddenly her heart felt lighter. Forget her vow to become independent, to stand on her own two feet. She hadn't felt this giddy since her high-school days when her prom date showed up, and it wasn't entirely because she needed a handyman around the house.

Opening the door, she resisted the urge to hug Logan Strong. Barely. "You, sir, are an answer to a woman's prayers."

A wicked smile slanted his lips, and he arched his brows. "I am?"

"Absolutely. Assuming you know anything about plumbing and you're here to work on my honey-do list." *Or take her out to dance the whole night through.*

He laughed, that warm chuckle that seemed to rumble through his chest and skitter along her flesh like a tropical mist. "Darn, and here I thought you had something else in mind."

Janice flushed. At some very conscious level, she *had* been thinking of something else—something forbidden—but she didn't want to admit that, certainly not to Logan. "I'm sorry. I mean, you said you might come back to..."

"I meant to come a couple of days ago, but I was studying for the engineers' exam that's coming up soon."

"Then you really don't have to—"

"Fixing busted plumbing is one of my all-time favorite things to do."

"It is?" She looked at him incredulously.

"Sure. It falls on my list of favorites somewhere

between cleaning out backed-up sewers and crawling through an attic crawl space on a blistering hot summer day.''

Delight fluttered in her midsection at his teasing tone. When was the last time she'd actually had fun with a man? So long ago she couldn't remember.

''Do you suppose there's a way I could clone you? Renting you out to distraught housewives would solve all my financial problems.''

With a welcoming smile, she opened the door and he stepped inside. Although he wasn't a giant, he was tall enough that she suspected he'd played high-school basketball. And he was lean, like a runner, with great shoulders and well-defined biceps apparent beneath the stencilled T-shirt he wore, a souvenir of a recent 10K run in Paseo. Today he was wearing khaki shorts. His knees weren't at all knobby, she noted. Instead, his muscular legs were worth writing home about.

''What seems to be the problem?'' he asked.

A vivid imagination on her part. Or maybe she was suffering from an extended case of celibacy. Since Maddie's birth, she hadn't been much interested in sex. To her relief—and occasional dismay—Ray hadn't pressed her. Now one look at Logan and that's all she could think about—hot, sweaty bodies. His and hers. Tangled sheets. An explosion of—

What she needed to think about was the swimming pool the plumbing had created in the laundry room.

''The washing machine.'' Her breath caught in her throat, making her voice sound husky. Hardly an appropriate reaction when discussing a home appliance.

"The connection has sprung a leak. Ray was supposed to—"

"Show me."

Mentally chastising herself for mentioning her late husband in a critical way, she led Logan to the laundry room off the kitchen. She told herself if Ray hadn't been so busy with his second job, he would have fixed the plumbing. But deep inside she knew that was a lie. He'd never been good around the house. She'd had to beg to get a new garbage disposal installed. The paint was peeling on the outside of the house, but Ray had never been interested in sprucing up the place. Only the garden, with rosebushes and beds of annuals, looked nice. That had been her own doing. She'd sunk a shovel into the dirt herself, added mulch and whatever else it took to make flowers bloom. Ray hadn't seemed to notice.

Just as he'd stopped noticing her.

Logan leaned over the back of the washing machine. "You're right. Looks like the hose has developed a split and the clamps are corroded. I'll need some parts from the hardware store."

"I can pay—"

"No, I'll take care of it. It's the least I can do."

His odd tone sent an unwelcome shiver down her spine. "Why is it the least you can do?"

He didn't meet her gaze. "I was on the roof with Ray when he fell. I owe him…and I owe you."

Janice's stomach knotted on that news. She hadn't asked the details about Ray's death, hadn't wanted to know. And didn't want Logan here out of obligation.

But she did want him *here*. His presence pervaded the house with a new energy, a force that was more than simply filling the silence that had been troubling her. He radiated strength of character. Competence. And a subtle sexual power she couldn't remember experiencing before.

The uncomfortable knot tightened in her midsection, and she couldn't find the words to respond to his comment. Instead, she said, "I have to go pick up Maddie from kindergarten in a couple of minutes."

He shoved aside the pile of towels she'd used as a dam. "Leave this Johnstown flood to me. Once I get the parts, it won't take long to fix."

She met his gaze, his eyes a deeper hazel than usual, almost brown, and unreadable. Or at least she didn't want to translate the message she saw there for fear she'd be wrong and make a fool of herself.

"It won't take me long to pick up Maddie. I'll be back in just a few minutes. The tools are in the garage if you need them." Janice fled. She'd never thought of herself as a coward. But she couldn't describe her flight in any other terms.

At some very basic level, Logan frightened her. Or more accurately, her reaction to Logan scared the bejeebers out of her. She'd never felt this way about any man, including Ray, with hot and cold shivers racing across her skin, the confusion that should be limited to inexperienced adolescents. She'd been a married woman for almost ten years. Such nonsense, so many raging hormones, should have been well behind her.

Minivans didn't usually burn rubber. But Janice wheeled out of the driveway so fast the tires squealed. Within two blocks she slowed, realizing she'd never be able to outrun her own wayward thoughts.

Junipero Serra Elementary School was a relatively new one, a sprawling one-story complex with two big play yards. Because of population growth, however, the school district had added four trailers for additional classrooms and there was talk of developing a new school on the north side of Paseo del Real to take the pressure off existing facilities. Taxpayers weren't thrilled with the idea.

Janice parked the van and walked toward the separate building that housed two classes of kindergartners. Smiling, she acknowledged other mothers who'd come to pick up their children, some of them pushing strollers or holding the hand of a toddler. Regret slid through Janice's chest at the thought she'd never have another baby to hold in her arms. Thank God Maddie had come along despite Ray's insistence that one child was enough.

The adjacent play yard for the kindergarten children had one corner blocked off with a yellow tape where a three-foot-deep construction pit had been dug to install a new piece of play equipment. Vaguely, Janice wondered if that bit of construction wouldn't have been better and more safely accomplished during the summer vacation. A yellow tape, like those used around crime scenes, hardly seemed strong enough to keep out curious children.

Like a cork on a bottle of champagne popping, the

classroom door flew open and a stream of five-year-olds burst free. Maddie was in the middle of the swarm. She made a beeline for Janice and flung herself into her mother's arms.

"Mommy!" she sobbed.

Kneeling, Janice caught her daughter. "What is it, sweetheart? Did you hurt yourself?"

"Uh-uh." She shook her head. Her eyes were red-rimmed and tears tracked down her cheeks.

"Then what—"

"Hello, Mrs. Gainer."

Seeking an explanation for her daughter's distress, Janice looked up at Miss Sebastian, the kindergarten teacher. Her youthful complexion and pert ponytail made her look as if she should still be in high school, not a second-year teacher.

"I told the students this morning about Daddies' Day in our classroom next week. I like to involve their fathers as much as I can in the children's education. I'm afraid that's what upset Maddie."

Janice drew a painful breath.

"My daddy's dead." Sobbing, Maddie mashed her face against Janice's shoulder.

"I tried to explain that grandfathers or uncles would be welcome, or any man who is special in their lives."

Standing, Janice lifted Maddie, and the child hooked her legs around Janice's waist. Her heart was breaking for her daughter. She hadn't realized Maddie's grief was still so raw. She was such a happy child, but now it was obvious the wound had only healed on the surface. Down deep, she was still hurting. Janice should have realized a month wouldn't be nearly long enough for her children to adjust to such a drastic change in their lives.

"I'm afraid our family is all in Missouri," Janice explained.

"Quite a few of the children don't have a father at home, or their father works at a job where he can't get off. Maddie won't be the only child without someone here that day. I'm sorry." Despite her youthful appearance, Miss Sebastian looked sincerely apologetic. "It had slipped my mind that you'd lost your husband so recently."

"We'll work out something. Maybe she can bring his picture—"

"No! I want my daddy!"

Pursing her lips, Janice hugged her daughter more tightly and fought her own tears. "Let's talk about this at home, honey. Okay? Logan Strong is there fixing our washing machine."

Maddie sniffled. "'Kay."

Janice gave the teacher a weak smile. "She'll be all right."

"I am sorry—"

Nodding, she carried Maddie out to the van. No doubt this would be just one of a long list of adjustments she and the children would have to make over the coming months and years. But they were strong. All three of them. They'd come through this just fine. Janice would see to that.

BY THE TIME Logan returned from the hardware store, Janice's van was back in the driveway. He parked out front and walked to the side entrance, carrying the supplies he'd purchased to repair the washing-machine hose.

The house showed lots of signs of deferred maintenance—peeling paint, bubbling stucco where water had seeped up from the ground, a swing out back with a broken chain. No doubt Janice's honey-do list could keep him busy for years.

A chance to see her smile or hear her laugh would keep him coming back even longer if he allowed that to happen. Which he wouldn't. Helping her transition to single mother was his only goal. Plus easing his own sense of guilt for not having acted to save Ray's life, he admitted.

He rapped on the door before stepping inside.

"Did you get everything you needed?" Janice stood at the kitchen counter making a sandwich.

"Yep." He held up the four-foot-long rubber hose he'd purchased. The necessary clamps were in a small sack he carried.

Maddie sat at the kitchen table, her chin propped on her elbows. She looked as though she'd had a really hard day at school.

"You want a sandwich before you start?" Janice asked. "I can give you a choice of peanut butter or tuna salad."

"I'm having peanut butter and jelly," Maddie said with a minimum of enthusiasm.

"Why don't I work on the washer first? It won't take me long."

He went about the business of pulling the washer

away from the wall so he could disconnect the old hose. Within minutes he sensed Maddie standing behind him.

He glanced over his shoulder. "What's up, sprite?"

"Nuthin'," she said glumly. "How come you call me sprite?"

"Because I think you're cute and bubbly."

She watched silently as he pulled off the old hose and connected the new one. As he attached the first clamp and started to tighten it with a screwdriver, he felt vaguely pleased she was interested in what he was doing. He remembered watching his father—

"Would you be my daddy?"

His head snapped up, nearly giving him a whiplash, and the screwdriver slipped from his hand, clattering to the floor. "What did you say?"

"I want you to be my daddy." She stood there with big brown eyes, as serious as an old woman.

"I think your mom might have something say about that."

"Say about what?" Janice asked, returning to the kitchen from wherever she'd been.

"Logan's going to be my daddy."

His gaze collided with Janice's. Her cheeks were turning as pink as his felt. "I don't know where she got—"

"Maddie, honey, I don't think Logan wants to—"

"But it's only for one day!"

His gaze dropped to the child. "What are we talking about?"

Janice stepped forward, looping her hands over her

daughter's shoulders and pulling the child back against her, holding her snugly against her own body. "Her teacher invited the children's fathers to a Daddies' Day at school next week. Maddie got terribly upset she didn't have anyone to bring."

"Oh." Odd how he wished Maddie's request had been for something more permanent. "Guess that is a problem."

"Not if you'll be my pretend daddy."

"Honey, Logan may have work that day, and even if he doesn't, he may have other things he wants to do."

Maddie's lower lip jutted out, and her eyes filled with tears.

Janice was providing him with all the excuses he could possibly need. But Logan couldn't turn down Maddie's request, not with those big soulful eyes pleading with him to be her daddy, if only for a few hours. Hell, no man would be able to resist such a tempting little minx.

He worked his way out from behind the washing machine and crouched down in front of her. "What day are we talking about?"

"Miss Sebastian said Wednesday."

Logan touched the tip of Maddie's nose with his fingertip, leaving a greasy smudge. "Well, you tell your Miss Sebastian I'll be there with bells on."

Maddie's eyes lit up and she threw her arms around him, giving him a gigantic five-year-old hug. "I knew you would 'cause firemens are special."

A lump filled Logan's throat, so big he could barely

swallow, and a band tightened around his chest. Among all the experiences he'd miss by not marrying, the thought of never having children hurt the most. Still, it was a choice he'd had to make after his one attempt at marriage.

Concerned he might be overstepping his bounds with Maddie, he glanced at the child's mother. Janice's eyes glistened with unshed tears as she mouthed, "Thank you."

His tension eased, and he relaxed his hug around Maddie's small body.

Clearing her throat, Janice said, "How about you change out of your school clothes, young lady, and let Logan finish up with the washing machine. We don't want to keep him here all day."

As though she hadn't been down in the dumps only moments ago, Maddie broke free of the hug, her smile radiant. "I'll change. Then I'll come help him. I helped him real good on the screen door."

"You certainly did," Logan agreed, regret gnawing through him for what couldn't be.

Janice rolled her eyes and leaned back against the doorjamb as her daughter ran off to change clothes. The child had more resilience than she did. More nerve, too.

"I don't want Maddie imposing herself on you, Logan." Janice had done plenty of that herself. "In time she'll get used to—"

"It'll be fun visiting her kindergarten. I like kids."

He was wonderful with them, too, she mused. "I

feel guilty taking you away from your own activities. Like studying for your engineers' exam.''

''I've been studying for months. I could use the break.''

''When's the test?''

''Two more weeks.'' Reaching down, he picked up the screwdriver, rolling it back and forth in his hand. He had long, tapered fingers, almost like an artist's. Hands that had been ever so gentle with her daughter. Just as his words had been.

''I gather you're ambitious?''

''My dad retired a year ago as a fire captain right here in Paseo. His shoes are big ones to fill, but making engineer is the next step. My brother and I are in a race to see who makes captain first.''

''Who's ahead?''

''Derek's on the promotion list now for engineer in Merced. I'll have to ace both the written exam and the oral to have any chance of making the grade before he does.''

''Somehow I think you'll do just that.'' She shoved away from the doorjamb. ''Here I was trying to get Maddie to stop bothering you, and now I'm the one bugging you with questions.''

''You'd never bug me, Jan,'' he said softly. ''Not ever.''

A tremor of pleasure rippled through her. ''I think I should…that is…'' She stumbled over her words, her unruly thoughts tangling with her good sense. ''I'm going to go wash Ray's car and vacuum it. I'm putting an ad in the paper and hope to sell it this weekend.

We still owe quite a bit on the loan. Owning a convertible is one expense I can do without.''

''Sounds like a smart move to me. You know how to price it?''

''I checked the Blue Book.''

''Good for you.'' Nodding his approval, he eased back behind the washer, crouching down out of sight.

Deliberately, Janice turned away. She wasn't going to make a big deal out of Logan's kindness to her daughter, or fantasize about the intriguing timbre of his voice and how it raised gooseflesh along her spine. Or even how Logan, unlike her husband, seemed to think she had enough intelligence to make a reasonable decision.

She was a recent widow. Logan obviously felt a loyalty to her late husband. That was all she had a right to expect. She shouldn't go looking for trouble.

Backing Ray's Chrysler convertible out of the garage, she parked it in the driveway. The car had been an extravagance in her view, but Ray had been insistent. The symptom of a mid-life crisis, she supposed. She'd given in easily enough. He worked hard and deserved a little fun. Admittedly, it was a spiffy car—fire-engine red with a glossy finish. But for her and the children, the aging minivan would do fine.

She got the hand-held Dustbuster from Ray's workbench. With the top down, it was easy to climb in and out of the car. She started with the driver's side, trying not to picture Ray sitting there, smiling so broadly because he'd gotten a new toy. Teasingly, he'd called

the convertible his "pickin' up chicks" car. She
hadn't been particularly amused.

She tossed the floor mats onto the grass to wash
later. The Dustbuster inhaled the collection of dirt and
sand easily, and she worked her way across to the
passenger side. She checked the glove box, setting
aside the registration and the owner's manual, vacu-
umed the carpeting on that side of the car, then
climbed into the back seat.

The upholstery looked virtually pristine, no wear
and tear evident at all. Thinking she ought to get a
fairly good price, considering the car's condition, she
ran the vacuum beneath the front seat. When she
brought the vacuum back into view, a piece of purple
fabric dangled from its mouth.

She switched off the power and sat up on the seat
staring at the swatch of nylon material. Her stomach
knotted in apprehension. Slowly she pulled the fabric
free.

Thong panties!

Could there be any *innocent* reason for another
woman's underwear to be in the back seat of Ray's
car?

Nausea rose in her throat. Could she have been so
stupid, so naive as not to know Ray was having an
affair?

She got down on her hands and knees, feeling
around under both front seats. Her fingers closed over
a small plastic tube. A lipstick.

Mango Madness! Never in her life had she worn

that shade of lipstick. It would make her look like a hooker.

Trying to breathe against the pain that speared through her chest, she closed her eyes. To her dismay, she pictured a woman who had been at Ray's funeral service. A stranger. Long blond hair. Dark glasses. Shockingly bright orange lips.

Outrage warred with the knowledge she had failed as a wife. As a woman.

Stomach heaving, she bolted from the car, collapsing on the grass near the flower bed she had so lovingly tended. She breathed deeply, desperately trying not to be sick.

Chapter Four

Wiping his hands on a rag he'd found, Logan stepped outside. He came to an abrupt halt when he spotted Janice kneeling beside a rosebush that was in full bloom, the hot summer sun casting her sable hair with highlights of red. Something told him she hadn't taken a break from washing the car just to smell the flowers.

"Jan? You okay?"

It was a long time before she looked up at him, her ginger-brown eyes bleak, her face as pale as death.

Grief, he realized, feeling a punch in the gut. She'd been cleaning up Ray's car and the memories must have overwhelmed her.

He hunkered down beside her. It was all he could do not to touch her, to soothe the frown from her forehead, to pull her into his arms to comfort her. But it wasn't his place to do that. He'd been the one to let her husband die when the tragedy could have been avoided if he'd acted promptly. He might never get past that guilt.

"Tough remembering, huh?" he asked.

To his surprise, she opened her hand that had been

closed into a fist. A skimpy bit of silky stuff appeared. A pair of women's undies, such as they were. Vibrant purple. As sexy as anything he'd ever seen.

He swallowed hard as the image of Janice wearing those thong panties leaped into his head.

"You found them in the car," he ventured, "and the memories—"

"They're not mine."

His mental picture shattered, the pieces separating like a child's cardboard puzzle tossed into the air.

"I'd never wear thongs. I'd hate them." Her whispered words rasped with pain. "I wear bikinis. White bikinis so I don't get a pantyline and they don't show through."

A new image appeared. More innocent. Even more desirable. But he knew her thoughts were going in a different direction, the evidence of infidelity.

She opened her other hand to show him a lipstick tube. "This isn't mine, either."

"There could be a reasonable—"

"He was having an affair."

"You don't know that for sure."

"She was at the funeral. I saw her." She shuddered, as though someone had walked over her grave.

Logan swore under his breath.

"Did you know?" she asked, her tone accusing. "Did he *talk* about her? *Brag* about his conquests?"

"Ray didn't confide in me. We weren't that close."

"You rode the ladder truck together. You must have talked—"

"No." He wasn't going to tell her what he knew,

though the questions he'd had that fateful morning now had some answers, ones that Logan didn't much like. Ray had been in Vegas with a woman—a woman who wore purple thong undies. He'd been hungover, if not still drunk, and exhausted by the drive home and very likely from a lack of sleep after carousing the whole weekend.

Mentally, he cursed Ray for a whole lot of sins, but mostly for hurting Janice.

Glancing away, Janice gazed at the budding American Beauty rose. The petals were perfect, not a sign of bug infestation, the color deep red. She sprayed her roses every other week from spring through summer, and fertilized just as often. The rest of her garden she tended with equal care.

Obviously she hadn't done as well at her marriage.

"I knew we had problems," she said softly. "I thought…I thought I'd still have time to make things right. We'd only drifted apart. He was working so hard—" She lowered her head. She didn't need to make excuses for Ray. She'd been willing to try. He hadn't. He'd found someone else.

The back door flew open and Maddie pranced outside wearing shorts and a crop top. "Can I help wash Daddy's car?"

Shoving the thong and lipstick in her pocket to hide the evidence of Ray's infidelity, Janice stood. Logan's hand at her elbow steadied her. Warm. Strong. Caring. What must he think of her? A woman who couldn't keep her husband from straying?

And what of the blonde? Would it do any good to

track her down, confront her? It seemed so pointless. Far too late to make a difference.

"Mommy?"

Dragging her thoughts back to the moment, Janice looked down at her daughter, and the sense of outrage returned. By being unfaithful to her, Ray had also been disloyal to their children. Her beautiful babies. For that she might never forgive him.

She squared her shoulders. "Of course you can help wash the car, honey. Do you remember where we keep the bucket and sponge?"

"I'll get 'em." Whirling away, Maddie skipped toward the garage, happy and carefree.

"I'll help, too," Logan said.

"I don't want the children to know about Ray's—" she had to swallow before she could force out the word "—infidelity."

"They won't hear it from me." The sympathy in his hazel eyes comforted her.

Placing her hand over his, she squeezed gently. "Thank you. For everything."

Washing a car with the assistance of a five-year-old was like taking an outdoor shower. More suds got on Maddie than on the car. Water sprayed everywhere, dousing them all and spattering the windows of the house. But there was laughter, too. Maddie's and Logan's. Despite the pain gnawing at her insides, Janice was able to smile.

They were doing the final polishing when Kevin arrived home pedaling his bike. Sliding to a stop, he dropped his bike onto the grass.

"Hi, honey, I thought you had soccer practice after school?"

"We can't have a team. There's nobody to coach us." Disappointment and anger rolled off him in waves as he took off his helmet and tossed it to the ground.

"But I thought—"

"Dad was gonna coach us this year. Then he went and died, and there isn't anybody else." He swiped at his eyes with the back of his arm.

"Your father said that?"

"He promised. Now everybody blames me 'cause we don't get to play."

Seeing Kevin's distress, Maddie went to him and wrapped her arms around him. "You can play with me," she volunteered.

Fighting tears, Janice pursed her lips, then drew a deep breath. Ray's death wasn't going to ruin her son's life. Or his budding soccer career. "I'll coach your team."

"Aw, Mom, you don't know anything about soccer." He pushed Maddie away but not with irritation. More like a macho refusal to show affection for his little sister in front of anyone else.

"Of course I do. Haven't I gone to every one of your games for the past three years? I know about off sides and goal kicks, penalty shots."

"You don't know about strategy. Stuff like that."

"What I don't know, I can learn." There had to be books about coaching.

"We'd probably lose every game."

"It'd be better than not playing at all, wouldn't it?" she argued.

Kevin was weighing that question when Logan rounded the car, wiping water spots from the hood with a soft rag.

Kevin eyed him speculatively.

In an effort to halt the thoughts that were so obviously whizzing through her son's head, Janice opened her mouth to speak. She was too late.

"Have you ever played soccer?" Kevin questioned.

"Sure." Wringing out the rag, Logan shrugged. "I was a striker when I was about your age, played some halfback, too."

"I would have guessed you played basketball," Janice commented, momentarily distracted by her earlier assumptions about his athletic talents.

"In high school. The year I turned fourteen, I shot up five inches in about three months. Drove my mother crazy buying me new pants. The basketball coach recruited me right out of gym class."

Unbidden, Janice's gaze slid to his legs. She could imagine his mother's frustration trying to keep him in long pants during a growth spurt. But the results were well worth admiring now with Logan wearing shorts.

"I play fullback," Kevin said. "I'm not real fast but I fight for the ball."

Logan smiled at the boy, that quiet smile he shared so easily. "That's half the battle."

"Could you coach my team? Mom would but she don't know much."

Logan's lips quirked in surprise and amusement.

Janice sputtered. "Kevin, you can't ask—"

"I couldn't commit to coaching every practice," Logan said. "You know what a firefighter's schedule is like. But maybe I could assist—"

"But Dad said—"

Janice looped her arm over her son's shoulder. Ray had made a lot of promises he couldn't keep, including one to love and honor her. "Logan's being very generous to offer his help. If you think the team could survive with your mother as coach and Logan assisting, maybe we could talk another dad into helping out, too."

"I guess."

Not exactly a vote of confidence, but she gave her son a squeeze anyway. "It'll work out." So would their lives, even with the painful knowledge that Ray had been unfaithful. Lots of women raised their children without the help of a man. She could do it, too.

Glancing up at Logan, seeing his understanding smile, her heart did a little flip. For now, at least, she wasn't on her own. Within the course of one day, Logan had fixed her washing machine, agreed to play the role of Maddie's father at kindergarten Dads' Day and volunteered to be the assistant coach for Kevin's soccer team.

Why was he being so kind? she wondered. And dare she read more into it than simply a firefighter helping out the widow of one of his fallen brothers?

At this point, with her emotions so volatile and her nerves pulled taut, she didn't know quite what to wish for. It would be far better if she'd simply concentrate on getting her life together and taking care of her family.

LOGAN TOOK a swipe at a drip of water that had seeped from beneath the convertible's door. He'd gotten himself in deep now.

He'd intended to help Janice out around the house, give her some room to adjust to being a widow, then back off again. Keep his distance.

Now he'd found himself volunteering to play Maddie's daddy, if only for a morning, and helping to coach Kevin's soccer team. That meant he'd be seeing Janice often. That meant he'd be tempted day after day, week after week for the entire soccer season, to take her in his arms, pull her slender frame against his chest. Kiss her.

Damn, he was already starting to sweat and it didn't have a lot to do with the temperature. For the sake of his sanity, he'd better start hoping now the team didn't extend the season by getting into the playoffs.

Seeking a distraction, Logan picked up the hose, twisted the nozzle open. "Hey, Kevin, you missed out on all the fun washing the car." The fine mist caught the youngster across the chest.

"No fair!" With a laugh, the kid dashed for cover behind the convertible. "You don't wanna get the car wet again."

With a teasing growl, Logan stalked after him. "Are you sure about that?"

"Can't catch me!" Maddie dared him, running away from Logan.

He squirted both children and welcomed the breeze that blew water back in his face, hoping the cold spray would cool him off.

Kevin outran the reach of the hose, stopping at the far side of the yard and grinning a new challenge at Logan. "Hey, why don't you get Mom!"

He shot a glance at Janice.

"No." She backed up a step. "You wouldn't."

"Your son seems to think it's a good idea."

Eyes wide, she retreated another few steps. "What's he know? He's only a kid."

"Get her, Logan!" Kevin shouted.

Her gaze flicked toward the back door, obviously searching for a way to escape. The corners of her lips quivered with the threat of a smile, and he really wanted to make her smile. The image of her sad, haunted eyes as she'd clutched another woman's panties in her hand remained vivid in his mind.

"A mother should be allowed to maintain her dignity in front of her children."

"Is that so?" He edged the spray of water closer to her feet.

With a cry, Maddie flew at him, wrapping her arms around his legs. "Don't hurt my mommy! Don't hurt her!"

Startled, he twisted the nozzle closed and knelt down to Maddie's level. "I'm not going to hurt her, sprite. I'd never hurt your mom."

In an instant, Janice was there with him, pulling her daughter into her arms. "It's all right, sweetheart. Logan was teasing me, that's all. Just like he was teasing you. We were all having fun.''

The child's lips trembled. "I didn't want him to make you cry. Like Daddy sometimes used to—''

"Shh, honey. It's all right." Janice met Logan's gaze over the top of her daughter's head. "I'm terribly ticklish. There were times when Ray—''

Logan shook his head. He didn't want to hear this. He knew what it was like to be tickled to the point of torture. He'd seen a bully in his neighborhood do that to a younger kid. Logan had jumped the older boy and pulled him off, at the cost of a cut lip.

He'd do the same thing now if he could have reached past the grave.

Anger, and the need to do something, anything, to make life easier for Janice, propelled him to his feet. "Hey, how 'bout I take us all out for pizza for dinner? After we get dried off.''

Kevin cheered.

"You don't have to do that," Janice said, still kneeling by her daughter.

"I want to," he said simply and walked away before his emotions slipped totally out of control. It was her vulnerability that got to him, along with her determination to be just the opposite. In the past, he'd sensed her hidden strength each time they'd met. A flash of stubbornness in her eyes, a subtle lift of her chin even when Ray had made a teasing remark that was hurtful. She'd refused to totally surrender the essence of herself to her husband. Now, in the face of new challenges, she wasn't giving in either.

That demonstrated the same courage it took to walk into a building filled with black smoke. It made her worthy of respect…and love.

A love Logan didn't have the right to offer.

JANICE PLUCKED a lone bite of pepperoni from the one remaining slice of pizza on the table. Logan had succumbed to the kids' request for quarters, and the children had gone off to play the electronic games. Kevin had been told to keep careful watch of Maddie, but from where Janice was sitting, she could easily see them both. She preferred it that way.

She glanced at Logan across the table from her. He seemed content with the silence between them. Despite his occasional teasing ways, he was a serious man. Oddly studious for a firefighter. Not at all the devil-may-care bachelor that Jay Tolliver and Mike Gables had been until their recent marriages. Someone who held in his emotions. A man she could rely on.

Perhaps that's why his silence felt comfortable. She didn't feel a need to be anything except herself. A single mother with two children who appreciated his friendship.

"I hope you're not being generous with both your time and your money because of survivor's guilt."

"Nope." His smile crinkled the corners of his eyes and to her delight, a crease appeared in his left cheek, a dimple of happiness she hadn't noticed before. "We're here because I'm addicted to pizza."

She forced herself to concentrate on the conversation instead of his slightly lopsided grin. "I thought you were totally into gourmet cooking."

"Everyone needs to go slumming once in a while."

She barked a very unladylike laugh. "Thanks a lot!"

"No, I didn't mean—" He leaned forward, covering her hand with his. "How about if I admit I enjoy your company? And your kids, too, of course. I think Ray was a fool to have even looked at another woman."

She felt a stab of pleasure, then chided herself for being flattered by his comment. For being so needy and vulnerable. He was probably only trying to make her feel better after the day's revelations. Doing a good job of it, too, she mused. Although no one would be able to soothe entirely the knot of pain Ray's infidelity had caused her, or the self-doubt that maybe she was partly to blame.

Regretfully, she slid her hand from beneath his.

"I want you to know I'd never blame you or anyone else in the department for Ray's death. Fighting fires is a dangerous business. It comes with the territory. Ray knew that. So did I. The business with the blonde—" Her gaze slid away from his so he wouldn't see the depth of her pain. Or her confusion because she felt she should be even more angry than she was. "That sort of blindsided me. I should have recognized the signs. His second job was so demanding."

As though not sure what to do with his hands, he toyed with his fork, practicing the magic trick he'd showed the children, pretending to bend the fork and straightening it again. "You sure he had another job?"

"He came home with cash periodically. Sometimes as much as a thousand dollars at a crack. He said he was getting paid under the table. His boss wanted to save taxes, you know."

"What was he selling?"

"I, ah... He was a little evasive about that." She wondered if all women with cheating husbands put their heads in the sand, or if she'd been the only fool. "But if he didn't have a job, where did he get the money?"

"When we were going through your credit-card records, I saw a lot of charges from Las Vegas."

"That was part of his sales terri—" Her jaw dropped open like a cartoon character's as realization dawned. "Gambling. He got the cash from gambling."

"I'd say that was a fair assumption."

She glanced toward the children. They were playing on the same game together, a pair of cars racing along side by side on an electronic highway that was weaving and bobbing in front of them. Janice felt suddenly sick to her stomach.

"At least he was winning," she said. "The extra money he brought home—"

"I'd say he would have been lucky to break even. Vegas thrives on losers who keep going back to make up their losses."

Covering her mouth with her hand, she groaned. Maybe that's why he hadn't paid the insurance premium. He'd already spent the money. Dear God, why hadn't she paid more attention to their finances?

Because Ray hadn't wanted her to. Worse, he'd been keeping secrets from her. Living a whole other life. How long had that been going on?

"I'm going to have to track down every one of those bank accounts we have—or had—to see if there's any money left in them. What a nightmare."

"You'll get it straightened out."

"Ray never thought I was smart enough to handle the books, or so he said. But he was lying, wasn't he? About everything."

"You're plenty smart enough."

With that simple statement of encouragement, he bolstered her spirits. "You know, I had almost two years of college when I dropped out to marry Ray. My grades were pretty darn good, too."

"What was your major?"

"Nothing very useful, I'm afraid. History. In retrospect, accounting would have been a better choice."

His lips slid into one of those smiles that brought a catch to her throat. "History wasn't exactly one of my favorite classes."

"I loved hanging out at the library poring through old books looking for some arcane fact that nobody else knows or cares about. I'd probably be pretty good at writing up trivia questions but not much else." Tired of the smell of cold pizza, she stacked their plates on the pizza pan, shoving the mess farther down the long picnic-size table.

"I can think of a lot of things you'd be good at."

Her head snapped up. Surely she hadn't heard Logan correctly, or at least had misinterpreted the low, throaty sound of his voice, the sexy way he'd spoken. There was no reason her heart should have skipped a beat or her breathing gone shallow on her. He wasn't being flirtatious. That wasn't his style. Besides, why would he be interested in her?

"How long were you married?" she asked. "Not that it's any of my business."

"Less than a year. We were far too young when we got married. I was a probie, just starting my probationary period, still feeling my way on the job." He paused while a busboy cleaned up their dirty dishes and gave the table a haphazard swipe with a dirty rag. "Torie didn't know what to do with herself on the nights I was working. Instead she just fretted about me, afraid I'd have a terrible accident. She started having really bad dreams and claimed she couldn't sleep while I was gone."

"Strangely, though I suppose all firefighters' wives know there's a chance their husband will die on the job, I more often pictured Ray jogging around the track at the park or working out down in the gym, not fighting a fire. I suppose that's some kind of a self-protective mechanism so I didn't go crazy with worry."

"Torie's inability to cope with my job wasn't exactly healthy, I suppose. But I don't plan to put another woman through that same ordeal."

Janice suspected if the right woman came along, he'd change his mind. Logan was so steady and down-to-earth, he should be a family man. A husband and father. But he was making it abundantly clear he had no plans to tie the marital knot anytime soon.

Neither did she, at least not until she proved to herself she could make it on her own. Then maybe, years from now, she'd consider marriage again. She hoped the next time around she'd find someone as steadfast as Logan.

''How about Torie? Is she still in the picture at all?''

''I heard she got married a couple of years ago—to a man whose idea of fun is watching reruns of old sitcoms. A regular couch potato.''

She choked and began coughing. ''She certainly isn't into risk-taking, is she?''

''A woman can have a lot to lose.''

''In Torie's case, I think she must have a high tolerance for boredom when it comes to men.'' With a shake of her head, Janice pushed her chair back from the table. She couldn't imagine trading a marriage to Logan for the sake of security alone. ''Let's see if we can stop the drain on your supply of quarters. It's time to get the kids home, and I've got to call the head of the soccer league to tell him Kevin's team has a couple of brand-new coaches.'' She eyed him across the table. ''Unless you've had a change of heart.''

Slowly, he stood, and her gaze followed him up to his impressive height. ''Once I make up my mind to do something, I generally follow through.''

Every instinct in her agreed that was true. He'd never go back on his word. He'd be loyal to a woman—or his friend—even at the cost of his life.

Once upon a time, despite the circumstances of their marriage, she'd believed that about Ray, too. Obviously she'd been wrong. In her case, intuition wasn't a reliable yardstick.

She'd be wise to remember that. And wise to keep in mind Logan's vow never to marry again.

A FEW MINUTES LATER, just as the summer sun dipped below the coastal hills and cast the neighborhood into twilight, Logan pulled his Mustang up to the curb in front of Janice's house.

"Hey, Mom, what's that guy doing with Dad's car?" Kevin tried to shove the passenger seat forward before Janice managed to open the door and get out.

"I don't know, son, but I intend to find out." From the looks of things, a tow truck had backed into the driveway, the driver in the process of hooking up the convertible to haul it away. *Stealing it.*

Fury ripped through her as Janice got out of the car. Damn it! She'd be happy enough to see Ray's grown-up toy gone, along with the reminder of his infidelity, but she needed the cash she'd get from selling the car. Needed it badly.

Logan was several steps ahead of her, striding toward the thief. "Something we can do for you, fella?"

The scruffy tow-truck driver with stringy gray hair combed over his bald spot and wearing half-zipped, sloppy work pants, lifted his hands. "Take it easy, mister. This is all legal. I've got the court order in my truck. I'm repossessing this baby and there's nothing you can do about it."

"You're what?" Janice cried.

"How 'bout I take a look at the papers," Logan said calmly. Despite his shorts and T-shirt, he was an imposing figure of a man as he kept walking forward. The tow-truck driver retreated a step.

"Mom, don't let him take Dad's car!"

She physically restrained Kevin before he went after the stranger, too. "Stay back, honey. I'll...I'll take care of this." Surely of all their bills, Ray would have kept up the payments on his precious car. *Unless he'd gambled away* all *of their money*. Dear God, what would she do if that was the case?

Maddie latched onto Janice's leg. "What's happening, Mommy? I'm scared."

Hobbled by both of her children, Janice could barely move. "Don't worry, honey. Everything will be fine." She never lied to her children. Now seemed like a good time to start.

Keeping a cautious eye on Logan, the interloper edged toward his truck. He reached inside the cab and produced some official-looking documents. "It's all here," he insisted. "You're months behind in payments. I can't do nothin' about it now, but if you wanna see the dealer after I haul the car off, maybe you can make a deal."

Logan made a show of studying the papers, but Janice knew deep down in her gut what he'd find. Ray hadn't been paying the bills. Any of them, she guessed.

"Let him take the car," she said with a dull sense

of failure. Why hadn't she known? Why had he lied to her? Betrayed her?

"But Mom!" Kevin whined.

"Hush, honey. We don't need Daddy's car anyway. We've got the van." She forced a smile that made her cheeks hurt and almost broke her heart. "You're not quite ready to drive yet. One car is plenty for us."

The keen disappointment in her son's eyes hurt even more than the knowledge of her husband's infidelity. How dare Ray hurt their son! How dare he betray them all!

Logan handed the man back his paperwork. "Can she get any personal possessions out of the car?"

"Sure." With a relieved look, the stranger gestured toward the car. "Help yourself."

"I got everything I needed this afternoon," Janice said. Given a choice, she would have burned the purple thong panties hours ago but the scent of melting nylon would have made her sick to her stomach.

She looped her arms protectively around her children. "Come on, guys, it's getting on toward your bedtime. Logan's going to make sure no one hurts your dad's car." She sent him a pleading look, and he nodded. "In the house, both of you," she repeated to the children.

They objected, but she herded them inside, talking to them about school the next day, asking if Kevin had done his homework, which she knew he had. Anything to keep them from hearing the creak of the tow truck lifting their father's car off the ground, pulling it out of the driveway, the throaty sound of the truck's transmission as it accelerated away with the convertible dangling behind it. God, Ray would have hated that.

It was his own damn fault!

Janice hadn't realized how much anger she'd been holding inside as she got her children into bed. Not grief but rage that Ray had left her. Deserted her. And dumped a world of problems on her shoulders that should have been his to solve.

She wanted to scream so badly her throat ached, but that would only scare the children...and she was terrified that once she started screaming she might not ever be able to stop.

Downstairs again, she whirled when the back door opened. Logan stepped inside.

His gaze swept over her with more caring, more concern than she'd ever seen in her husband's eyes.

"I keep asking you if you're all right," Logan said, "and that's got to be the dumbest question of all."

Without requesting permission, he crossed the room and took her in his arms. He was warm and strong, his body lean and muscular. She clung to him as though he were a life raft in a stormy sea. She desperately wanted to be independent, succeed on her own. But for the moment, she needed someone, needed to be weak. Later, she told herself, she'd be strong. She'd find a way to survive. But not right now.

Her body quivering with a raw mixture of anger and need, she inhaled deeply. Logan's spicy scent. The residual smell of car soap. And something that was uniquely his own—tough and masculine, heroic yet amazingly gentle.

Forcing herself to lean away, she looked up into hazel eyes so dark they had become a deep brown. Her hands rested on his biceps. So strong. Powerful. She fought the urge to wrap her arms around his neck, kiss him. Invite him into her lonely bed.

She hadn't realized how much she'd missed being held. Being intimate with a man.

"God help me," she murmured, her feminine need and what she saw in his eyes warring with her good reason. It had been years since she'd responded to a man this way, that achy sensation of need building from somewhere deep inside.

Forcefully, she put that thought aside and tried to focus on the myriad problems she faced. "After all of this, I've got this awful feeling another shoe is going to drop."

Chapter Five

Two days later, Janice shaded her eyes with her hand to watch Logan walking across the schoolyard toward the soccer field. He had the look of a long-legged, loose-limbed cowboy, but she knew on a playing field or in a crisis he'd act swiftly. No question, she could get seriously addicted to seeing the man in shorts. Odd that she'd never realized what fascination muscular legs held for her.

Kevin and his teammates were jogging around the field to warm up before the scheduled practice. Logan said something to them as they passed him by, and the boys picked up the pace. He kept strolling toward her.

"Hey, coach," he said as he drew closer.

His easy, sexy smile made her wonder if all of his body parts, including his sensual lips, held a special interest for her. Kissable lips, neither too thick nor too thin, and she shouldn't be thinking like that. "Hi, yourself."

"Looks like you've got things underway."

"The league director loaned me a book—first

warm-ups, then basic skills like dribbling and passing. After that we can have a scrimmage.''

"Bet the guys would rather start playing right off.''

"They'd pull muscles if they didn't warm up first,'' she said confidently. After all, she'd already read through chapter three. "So I laid down the law to them. My way or the highway.''

He grinned at her. "You're gonna make a great coach.''

"Oh, you—'' She took a half-hearted swing at him, her hand connecting lightly with his arm. "You were pulling my leg, weren't you?''

"Now there's an idea with a lot of merit.''

A flush stole up her neck to heat her cheeks. She had no right to react to him this way. She had enough problems without asking for more trouble—man-woman trouble she was no expert at handling.

Before she spoke again, she glanced across the schoolyard to where Maddie was playing on the climbing apparatus with a couple of neighborhood youngsters—safe and unaware of the turmoil that had been roiling through Janice the better part of the day. Then she turned back to Logan.

"The other shoe dropped today.'' She tried to say the words lightly, as if the entire remainder of her world hadn't collapsed on her with the mail delivery.

A neat V formed between his brows. "What shoe?''

"A letter came for Ray from a Las Vegas casino. It seems he had rotten luck at the tables. He was in the hole almost as much as his state death benefit.''

She named the six-figure amount of Ray's gambling

debt, and Logan swore. "How can that be? Who the hell extended him that much credit? Firefighters don't make that kind of money. Somebody should have stopped him."

"Evidently that's not the casino's policy. And I hope to God Ray played at only *one* casino."

"Maybe you're not liable—"

"The letter was very threatening—just short of broken knee caps, reading between the lines. I don't think anyone gets off the hook simply by dying." She folded her arms across her chest as if she could stop the terror from building within her. Her life had turned upside down, her security vanishing like water through a sieve. At the rate bad news kept pummeling her, there was a real possibility she and her children would be homeless. But she had to hold on. Her kids were depending on her.

She lifted her chin. "The good news is if they take everything I have left I can declare bankruptcy and start over."

Logan swore again.

The soccer team rounded the last turn on the field and descended on the coaches. Most of the youngsters were breathing hard. Logan figured conditioning should be high on the list of things to do. Winning a close game in the fourth quarter could depend on it.

Coolly, as if she hadn't just announced a financial bombshell, Janice introduced Logan to the team. He tried to focus on remembering the kids' names. No easy task when he was still trying to absorb the news that anyone could run up a debt as large as Ray's.

With equal efficiency, she organized the boys into two relay teams and set them to dribbling the ball around Day-Glo-orange cones. Then she stood back to observe the action.

"What are you going to do?" he asked.

She glanced up at him. Her eyes were clear though troubled, her lips pulled into a determined line. "There's only one thing I can do. Well, two, actually. The only asset I have left is the house. There's no way I can meet the monthly mortgage payments, so I'm going to sell it." Her chin trembled ever so slightly. "And then I'm going to get a job and support my kids if I have to scrub floors seven days a week to do it."

Unable to resist, he brushed his fingertips across her cheek, caressing her smooth, perfect complexion. "What about your family? Couldn't they help?"

"They have their own problems. Besides, they're all in Missouri. This is my home, where I want my children to grow up."

"Then you'll manage. I'm sure of it."

She moved away from him as though unable to handle any show of sympathy at the moment. He gave her points for that. She was stronger than she realized, more determined. A hell of a woman.

"My biggest problem right now is that I hate to sell the house in its current condition. The exterior trim's a mess, the interior walls haven't had a coat of paint in years, the carpets could use a good cleaning—"

"We'll have a work party."

Her head snapped up. "What?"

"C-shift has a long weekend coming up. I'll get

everyone to pitch in." He didn't argue with her decision to sell the house. With only a small monthly income from Ray's pension and few other resources, that sounded like a reasonable decision. "The guys can sandblast the outside, paint and redo the trim, while the wives are working on whatever needs doing inside."

"I couldn't ask—"

"Of course you can."

"They were all so kind when Ray died—bringing casseroles, watching the children while I made arrangements. I can't ask—"

"They'll all be glad to help out now, too. They've probably been waiting to be asked to do something useful. You'll see." Logan couldn't ask them directly. He was still afraid they'd see the truth about Ray's fateful day in his eyes. But he could go to Chief Gray. When he found out Janice was in trouble, he'd get the men and their families to step forward. Logan could keep his distance. No one would realize he was trying to make amends for his lack of judgment.

One of the boys kicked the ball, and it came sailing full force right toward Janice's head. Logan reached out to fist it away goalie-style.

She gasped, belatedly ducking.

"Easy, fellas. That's a really important part of the lady's anatomy." He touched her arm gently in a reassuring gesture—both to tell her that she was safe and that she wasn't alone—though he would have liked to do far more. Not a good idea, considering the circumstances and the youthful audience. But he couldn't get the memory of holding her out of his mind. She'd felt so good, so right, snuggled up close to him. She'd fit in other ways too, ways he didn't dare contemplate in specific detail, not in front of the same pre-adolescent audience.

''The guys are getting restless,'' he said. ''Let's run them through some defensive drills.''

She nodded, gratitude in her eyes.

Damn, she was a strong woman. Not a lot of people—men or women—could take as many blows as she'd had to absorb lately and keep on standing. The fact that she kept fighting back was even more admirable.

As the practice progressed, Logan tried to focus on the kids' skills, making mental notes of which positions they'd fill best. That was no easy task. Watching Janice encouraging the boys, giving them quick hugs, and being instinctively loving was a distraction.

So was the way her tank top bared her shoulders to the sun, providing a target he had a desperate urge to kiss. Just a quick brush of his lips to feel their softness. A tiny bite to taste the sweet-salty flavor of her skin.

When they sent the boys on a final lap of the playing field, Logan went with them. He needed to work off a mountain of tension. He doubted one lap would do it.

After the players had left the practice field, and Logan was stuffing the soccer balls in their bags, he felt a tug on his shorts. Maddie's tiny, muddy hand, had grabbed hold of the hem.

''Hey, sprite, what's going on?''

"Can you bring Buttons to kenner-garden when you visit?"

"Uh, I don't know. You're sure it's okay?"

"Miss Sebastian said so. Charlie Greene is bringing his iguana. Buttons is lots prettier."

"I guess I'd have to agree with that." Fortunately, taking Buttons into a classroom wouldn't be a problem. The dalmatian often went along on fire-prevention visits to local schools and got far more attention from the students than the firefighter who accompanied the dog. "I'll check with the chief, okay?"

She beamed him a smile as if she'd known all along he'd do anything she asked of him. When she grew up, she was going to drive the boys crazy.

THE NEXT DAY at the fire station, Logan showered following the morning physical training session, then dressed and headed toward the chief's office. Councilwoman Evie Anderson waylaid him in the hallway. An attractive widow in her sixties, she showed up more frequently at the station than her position on the city council would warrant. Logan and the other firefighters figured she had a thing going for the chief, who was also widowed. They weren't equally convinced Harlan Gray reciprocated the councilwoman's feelings.

She extended a plate of homemade date-nut squares toward him. "Try one of these, dear boy. They tell me you're the best cook in the department. I'd value your opinion. It's a new recipe I'm trying. Harlan mentioned he liked dates.''

Logan swallowed hard. Based on past experience, he suspected Mrs. Anderson's recipe book had been written by the authors of *Arsenic and Old Lace.* ''Gosh, Mrs. Anderson, I've been trying to watch my sugar intake—''

''Oh, nonsense. That's what Harlan is forever telling me. You boys are all in such good shape, a little sugar won't hurt you. Besides, these are sugar-free.'' Selecting a cookie, she pressed him to take it. ''One bite, just to see if it's all right. Ever since I hit my head slipping on the city hall steps, I feel like I'm leaving ingredients out of my recipes. And my taste buds just aren't as reliable as they used to be.''

With a sigh, he took the cookie. Sacrifice was supposed to be good for the soul, he reminded himself grimly.

He took the tiniest bite he thought he could get away with. It stuck to the roof of his mouth. ''Chewy,'' he commented.

''But how does it taste?''

With a heroic effort, he swallowed and stopped himself from wincing at the bitter aftertaste. ''Ma'am, is it possible you substituted baking powder for baking soda?''

''Well, I don't know…they did seem to puff up a bit. Maybe I read the recipe incorrectly.'' Her pale-blue eyes widened. ''Oh, dear, if I did they'd taste terrible.''

Honesty was not necessarily a virtue, in this case, but he didn't know how to avoid it. "Yes, ma'am."

Her eager expression crumbled, the deep creases around her mouth formed by her perpetual smile vanished. "I've been thinking about having my eyes checked, but I've always been so vain about wearing glasses."

"You'd look very attractive in glasses, ma'am. Distinguished."

"Truth is, I'd rather be thought of as alluring by a certain gentleman. I haven't managed that little trick yet." She struggled to smile again. "At least you saved me the embarrassment of forcing these cookies on Harlan and the rest of you boys. Thank you for that."

"You're welcome, ma'am. I'm sure if you try again using baking powder they'll be fine."

She patted his arm, blue veins mapping the back of her hand. "Such a sweet boy. It's reassuring for the city to know brave young men like you are on the job protecting us."

"All part of the job, ma'am." He edged away from her. "If you'll excuse me…" Giving her a wave of his hand, he hurried down the corridor, glad to have escaped without hurting Mrs. Anderson's feelings too much…and without getting himself poisoned.

He rapped on the chief's door, entering when he heard the command, "Come in."

"Got a minute, chief?"

"Sure." Harlan looked past Logan's shoulder.

"Unless you're delivering a plate of cookies," he said under his breath.

Logan swallowed a smile. "No, sir. I believe the plate went back home again for a second try. Seems she didn't quite have the ingredients right."

With a sigh, the chief leaned back in his chair. Except for a file folder, a yellow pad of paper, some pencils and a photo of his family, his walnut desk top was clear of clutter.

"Thank goodness," he said. "Evie is the best-intentioned woman I've ever known, but I swear she's determined to give us all food poisoning."

"The men are pretty well onto her. I think we're safe."

"But am I?" he muttered under his breath.

"You might consider, if she shows up wearing glasses one of these days, uh, saying something nice about how they look on her. I think it might improve her cooking."

"Really?" His brows shot up, and he laughed. "I'll keep that in mind. Now, what can I do for you, Strong?"

"It's about Janice Gainer, Ray's wife."

Chief Gray immediately sobered. "Hell of a tragedy. I don't like losing my men." He leaned forward again, picked up a pencil and toyed with it. His graying brows pulled together and he looked directly into Logan's eyes. "How are you coping since the accident?"

"Fine, sir. Just fine."

The chief's eyes narrowed. "We can get you some counseling, Strong, if you're still having—"

"I'm not having any problems. I'm just concerned that Janice, Mrs. Gainer, is facing some difficulties. I thought the men would like to help."

"Why don't you ask them yourself?"

"It'd be better if it came from you, sir."

"Listen, Logan, I know you're planning to take the engineers' test, and you're well qualified. But lately you've been distancing yourself from the other men. That's not good if you want to move up in the ranks— and it could have an impact on the promotion list."

Logan struggled not to flinch—or argue. Damn it! He wanted that promotion. Needed it. His father didn't want anyone to know, but his retirement hadn't been all that voluntary. He had cancer. Big time. More than anything, Logan wanted that engineer's badge before his father died. He wanted his dad to know another member of the Strong family was moving up the departmental ranks in Paseo. Logan's brother felt the same way about his promotion in Merced. A family tradition.

But he couldn't tell anyone—not even the chief— what had happened that day on the roof.

When Logan remained quiet, the chief said, "During the debriefing you didn't shed much light on what caused the incident. Have you remembered anything since?"

"Everything was moving pretty fast." And what Logan did know would destroy Ray's image as a hero in the eyes of the department—and in the eyes of his children. Logan wasn't going to do that. Though knowing what a mess Ray had left his wife in, Logan figured that was more than the man deserved.

Not looking entirely pleased with Logan's evasive response, the chief nodded. "What seems to be Mrs. Gainer's problem?"

"She's going to have to sell her house." He went on to explain a few of Janice's problems as well as the need to spruce up the house.

"The death benefits ought to have covered—"

"They weren't enough to handle the debts."

The chief's scowl deepened. Swiveling, he checked the calendar on the wall behind his desk with the color-coded indication of what days which shift was on duty, then swung back. "C-shift and A-shift are off next weekend. I'll spread the word Mrs. Gainer needs help. Tell her I'll pick up the tab for paint, whatever it costs."

"I'd already planned to handle that personally, sir."

Harlan's brows slowly rose. "Are you two—"

"Ray was a fellow firefighter. That makes her a member of the family."

Logan wasn't sure the chief bought that line; he appeared to suspect something more was going on.

There wasn't, Logan told himself a few minutes later as he went upstairs for lunch. He didn't dare allow there to be.

The rest of C-shift parted for him like the Red Sea as he walked into the kitchen to scoop up what was left of a pasta chicken salad and find himself a roll. He'd been keeping his distance for so long, the men had begun to do the same. So much so, it might cost him the promotion he coveted. He tried not to worry about that.

The important thing was to get Janice some help fixing up the house so she could get a decent price for the place.

"MOM? Are you busy?"

With a sense of relief, Janice turned from the daunting task of cleaning out Ray's side of the closet to find out what her son wanted. She knew her reprieve wouldn't last long. With the necessity of selling the house soon, she'd have to box up a lot of her past. It wasn't going to be easy, and she wasn't looking forward to any new discoveries of Ray's infidelity.

"I thought you were getting ready for bed," she said, noting Kevin was still fully dressed. She'd tucked Maddie under the covers an hour ago.

"I was, but I had a question I wanted to ask."

That sounded serious since nine-year-old boys sought most of their answers from their peers. Or maybe their fathers.

Sitting on the edge of her king-size bed, she patted a spot beside her. He plopped down, letting his legs swing free.

"What did you want to know?" Mentally she ran through her store of knowledge on male anatomy and puberty. Wasn't Kevin too young for—

"Logan and Dad were friends, weren't they?"

Her brain skidded to a halt as she changed directions. "They rode together on the ladder truck for the past couple of years,'' she answered cautiously, unsure where this conversation might lead.

''Then do you think Dad would mind if I started to like Logan? You know, as a guy?''

Her heart did an unexpected tumble. She hadn't realized how eager her son was to have a masculine role model in his life. ''I'm sure your father would be very pleased for you to have another man to look up to.''

''He's pretty cool. Logan, I mean.''

She smiled. ''Yes, he is.''

''You like him?''

More than she ought to. ''He's been very kind to us,'' she hedged.

''Yeah.'' The boy hopped off the bed. ''I just didn't want to do anything that would make Dad mad, you know?''

She snared him by the hand before he could leave. ''Honey, you can't make your father angry no matter what you do. He's gone. What you have to do now is listen to your own heart. If you like Logan and want to look up to him, then that's exactly what you do. He's a fine man.''

Kevin gave her an embarrassed, little-boy smile and shrugged. ''I guess.''

''Come here, young man.'' Tugging him closer, she hugged him. ''I love you, Kevin.''

''Love you, too, Mom.'' Quickly getting his fill of maternal affection, he squirmed away and ran from the room. His footsteps pounded heavily down the hallway, then his bedroom door slammed behind him.

Janice winced. It was so easy to give her son advice. Not so easy to listen to it herself.

She pressed her fist against her midsection as a mixture of grief, anger and confusion welled up in her. To her dismay, the grief she felt was more because of the loss of her dreams than the death of her husband, her anger more for her children than herself.

The other emotions she'd been experiencing of late were far more difficult to define—her feminine awareness of Logan on every level from lust to admiration. Her need to be independent at exactly the same moment she wanted to throw herself into his arms and weep.

Her fear that she wouldn't be able to support and protect her children.

This was not the time in her life to develop a relationship with a man, even assuming Logan would be interested. She was too vulnerable. Too much was changing too fast.

But dear heaven, it would be so much easier if she, like Kevin, could take her own advice and simply listen to her heart.

MADDIE'S SMALL HAND slid into Logan's as they stood in front of the kindergarten class, Buttons beside him, tail wagging. The rest of the students were sitting on the floor, most of them cross-legged, looking up at them. A few couldn't manage to sit still for two seconds.

"This is Logan Strong," Maddie said in a big, five-year-old voice. "He's special 'cause he's a firemens.

Buttons is special, too, and I'm gonna get one of his wife's babies.''

"Puppies," Logan corrected. He and Janice had explained to Maddie that Buttons and Suzie were "married" lest she start asking questions that were too difficult to answer.

Maddie jutted out her chin in a stubborn gesture not unlike her mother's. "It's the same thing."

"Thank you, Maddie," Miss Sebastian said. "We appreciate having Firefighter Strong and Buttons visit our class. Now who else would like to introduce their special person?"

So much for Daddy show-and-tell, Logan thought with a grin. He resumed his seat next to Maddie, the low chair forcing him to pull his knees up practically to his chin. Buttons curled up comfortably beside him. Despite Logan's awkward position, he couldn't remember feeling so proud. He liked the idea of being Maddie's daddy, if only for an hour or so.

He shouldn't get used to it, though. Janice would get her life back together soon enough. Some other man would come along, and he'd earn the right to be Maddie's father.

And Janice's husband.

A muscle flexed in his jaw. Logan didn't like that idea and there wasn't a damn thing he could do about it.

ARRIVING EARLY to pick up Maddie, Janice strolled through the schoolyard with another kindergarten mother, who appeared to be about nine-and-a-half-months pregnant.

"Any day now?" Janice asked.

"Lord, I hope so. I'm so tired of carrying these two bowling balls around, I could die."

"Twins?"

The woman rolled her eyes. "My second set. They run in my family."

Janice laughed, wondering if she should offer condolences or congratulations. Her sympathy was with the poor woman, who looked desperately uncomfortable as she waddled across the schoolyard. Janice started to introduce herself just as the bell rang to announce the dismissal of the kindergarten classes.

The doors burst open, five-year-olds exploding from the room like skyrockets on the Fourth of July. In the middle of the chaos, Logan stood tall, Maddie at his side leading Buttons on a leash. Janice's heart did a tumble. Logan was such a beautiful man—

A scream that every mother recognized as a child in terror and pain wrenched through the air.

One of the kindergarten boys had fallen into the construction pit, a steel reinforcing bar piercing his thigh clear through, pinning him like a desperate butterfly.

Oh, dear God!

Janice had barely registered the scene and comprehended the crisis when she saw Logan race to the boy's side. He knelt, silencing the child almost instantly with a gentle hand and calm voice. Taking the boy's shoulders, he held him steady in his lap.

He looked up at the nearest adult. "Get to the office. Call 911 and tell them we need a fire rescue truck and an ambulance. Got that?" When the woman didn't budge, he said, "Go. Now. And come back to tell me how long till they'll get here."

Finally, wide-eyed, the woman reacted to his command.

As Janice reached the site, the child began to sob again. Logan was cradling him gently, blood oozing from the wound onto the leg of his uniform pants.

"Jan, get these children to back away. If their moms aren't here yet, have the teacher take them into the classroom. They don't need to see this."

She obeyed his order without question. She grabbed Maddie's hand. "Okay, kids, Miss Sebastian wants you back in the classroom right now." Noticing a few men among the clutch of children, she said, "Dads, can you help me out here?" That seemed to shake them from their temporary paralysis. Unlike Logan, they were ordinary men unused to responding to emergencies on a daily basis.

"Mommy, I wanna watch Logan," her daughter pleaded.

"Not now, honey."

"But Buttons—"

Janice took the dalmatian's leash from her daughter. "Why don't we take the dog back into the classroom, too? I bet he knows some tricks your friends would like to see."

The woman who'd made the phone call to 911 came

running back. "Two minutes," she announced breathlessly.

Janice could already hear the sirens on Paseo Boulevard. *Thank God!*

Logan nodded his acknowledgement but he didn't look up from his efforts to keep the injured child still and halt the bleeding. The ugly length of rebar looked like a spear jutting up from the boy's thigh.

Her heart doing an adrenaline mambo in her chest, Janice ushered the gawking, terrified children back toward the classroom.

"What's going to happen to Brandon?" her daughter wanted to know.

"Logan will take care of him. Right now, we have to keep out of his way so he can do his work."

Once in the classroom, Miss Sebastian took over. Although it was obvious she was shaken by what had happened to her student, she responded calmly, sorting out the children as their parents appeared at the door. The expectant mother of twins hung around, too, and it turned out she'd been a teacher at another Paseo school until she was simply too uncomfortable in her pregnancy to teach.

Janice kept glancing outside. The rescue personnel arrived a minute before Brandon's mother. Janice heard Logan reassuring the worried woman and giving softly spoken orders to the medical personnel. The men responded to his suggestions, following his leadership without question, just as Janice had. He was very much in command, and so in control in a crisis it amazed her. If anyone deserved a medal for heroics, he did.

And he was prepared to react in the same calm, deliberate manner to an emergency every day he put on his uniform.

Within a half hour, virtually all of the kindergarten children had been picked up by their parents or their daycare providers, and the injured child had been cut loose from the rebar. He was being ferried on a stretcher to the ambulance, his mother at his side, when the expectant mother of twins bent over double, moaning.

"What's wrong?" Janice asked.

"My water—" She gasped again. "Labor. I think my babies—"

Janice muttered an indelicate word. "Maddie, stay here. I'll get Logan."

She raced into the play yard, coming to a halt in front of him. Concern still pinched the corners of his eyes, and his pants were stained by a dark-brown swath of blood. "Can you handle a second crisis?"

"You're kidding."

"One of the kindergarten mothers has gone into labor."

He lifted his shoulders in a shrug. "No problem. There should be plenty of time to—"

"She's having twins. Her second set. From the look of her, I suspect it's going to happen in a hurry."

He grimaced. "Call 911."

"I'm on my way."

When she returned to the classroom, Logan had the

expectant mother—whose name was Alice Marie—lying on a gym pad, resting comfortably, calm now with his quiet reassurance. She'd make it to the hospital in plenty of time.

Miss Sebastian had Maddie and the older twins engaged in "training" Buttons to shake hands and roll over. A new set of paramedics arrived along with a second ambulance, and so did the expectant dad.

After everyone had left, Janice collapsed onto a kid-size chair in the classroom. She felt totally drained, every ounce of adrenaline having flowed through her body and out again.

"How do you do this every day?" she asked Logan, who was sitting on the floor leaning back against the wall beneath the chalkboard, casually petting Buttons. Strands of sandy-brown hair had shifted across his forehead. With an unconcerned gesture, he combed them back with his fingers.

"Some days we don't do anything at all. Then, bam! Four seconds and we're up to full speed. It can be a little hard on the heart," he admitted.

What was hard on Janice's heart was seeing Logan so competent, so totally in charge. It gave her shivers to think what might have happened to that child—and to the expectant mother—if Logan hadn't been here.

"Why don't you come home with me? I'll see if I can get that blood out of your pants."

"Actually, I've got an extra set of clothes in my car. I'll change, then I thought I'd go to the hospital, see how the kid is doing. I'll probably check in on the new mom, too, to make sure she's okay. The pants can wait for the cleaners.''

Janice's heart filled with an emotion she was afraid to study too closely. How many other men could cope with two emergencies one after the other, and their next thought was for the well-being of the victims they'd helped?

A man like that was worthy of a great deal. Including her love.

Chapter Six

She couldn't keep track of Maddie. Kevin was some-where outside, scraping paint off a windowsill, work-ing alongside the men, and Janice was afraid he'd fall off the stepladder he was using.

The entire crew of firefighters, their spouses—even Chief Gray's twenty-something daughter, Stephanie, who was home from her job in San Francisco for the weekend—were crawling all over her house, inside and out, like a swarm of busy ants. Despite their ob-jections that she didn't need to lift a finger, Janice had wielded a roller and brush, spattering her clothes in the process. In between she'd made three big pots of coffee, which had been quickly consumed. She didn't want to be treated as if she were fragile, unable to carry her own weight.

At the same time, she worried she wasn't acting the part of the grieving widow in front of Ray's friends. Well, they didn't know the whole story, did they?

But their generosity, their caring, was enough to bring tears to her eyes.

As she set another pot of coffee on to brew, she

realized that for the past ten years, she'd been the one to carry the emotional burdens for her family. Caring for the children. Being supportive of her husband, though she'd obviously failed in that regard.

Even as a child, she'd had to watch out for her younger siblings. Doctor their skinned knees. Listen to their troubles. Her mother had simply been too busy handling the large household to focus on Janice's specific needs.

Now a group of casual friends, her husband's co-workers and their family members, were showing her more compassion than she could ever remember experiencing. They astounded and touched her with their outpouring of goodwill.

Emma Jean swept into the kitchen. A big blob of antique-white paint clung to one of her dangling earrings, and there was a streak of the same color in her hair, which had not been added as a dramatic highlight by any beautician.

"We're about done with the second bedroom upstairs," she announced. "But I think that pink bathroom is going to need a second coat."

"All of you have been so wonderful...."

"Oh, I saw this coming. I mean...I was reading my tarot cards the other night and everything was a jumble. What else could that have meant except that we were having a work party?"

"Yes, well..." Janice never knew quite how to react to Emma Jean's announcements, most of which appeared to be plucked from the air. "Still, I appreciate everything you and the others are doing for me and my children.''

''No problem.'' She moved across the room with a soft chime of silver-on-silver and poured herself a mug of coffee from the fourth pot of the day. ''I was a bit confused when the knaves kept changing places. Then I realized that was only because Ray was still restless in his afterlife. He seems to have settled down now and is quite happy you and Logan will be marrying.''

Jaws are not supposed to drop to the ground, except in cartoons. But for all practical purposes, that's exactly what Janice's did.

''I—I beg your pardon?'' she stammered.

Lifting her mug in a toast, Emma Jean took a sip of coffee. ''Actually, at Mike Gables's wedding I noticed you and Logan together. I'd say the whole affair was fated from the beginning.''

''No. You're wrong. We're just…there isn't any…''

Andrea Peterson, the wife of the man who'd replaced Ray on the ladder truck, swept into the kitchen. Unlike Emma Jean and Janice, she didn't have a single spatter of paint on her. Indeed, she appeared to be a Martha Stewart look-alike who preferred to organize projects rather than get her own hands dirty.

''By chance, do you have any bottled water?'' Andrea asked, a sweet smile on her face. ''All the paint fumes are drying my throat, don't you know.''

''I'm sorry, I don't—''

Emma Jean brushed past Janice, coffee mug in hand. ''Don't you worry about a thing, hon. The cards are absolutely in your favor. My crystal ball is still a little murky, but don't let that bother you. I'll get the hang of it yet.''

Doing a mental blink, Janice watched the dispatcher walk out the door. No way was there marriage in her future, not anytime soon. And not with Logan, forget how she reacted to the man at a visceral level. That couldn't be in anyone's cards.

She was still dealing with too many other problems. Logan had been on the roof with Ray that fatal day. If Logan had any feelings for her, she was convinced it was more out of guilt than any sexual attraction. Next time around, when she made a commitment to a man, she wouldn't settle for less than—

''Water?'' Andrea asked. ''Perrier is what I prefer, but anything will do.''

Janice swung her head around. ''Tap water. I'm sorry, that's all I have. It's really quite tasty.'' She didn't have a clue why people drank out of those little bottles all day. As far as she was concerned, water was water.

''Oh, well, in that case...'' With considerable delicacy, Andrea picked up a glass that was on the counter, washed it out under the faucet, then filled it with water.

''I've got ice,'' Janice offered.

''This is fine. Thank you.'' She drank deeply. ''I don't think I've expressed my condolences properly for your loss.''

''It's all right. Just being here tells me you care.'' It also, on some level, gave Janice the creeps. Despite her vacillating emotions, she still didn't like the thought of anyone replacing her husband on the job he'd claimed to have loved. "Thanks for coming."

Andrea leaned back against the tile counter. Her dark hair was tied back in a tight bun, her high cheekbones highlighted with a perfect application of makeup. "I imagine Logan Strong was the first one here today."

At the peculiar tone of the woman's voice, Janice's eyebrows slammed down into a scowl. "He came early, yes. Is that a problem?"

"Oh, no, of course not. I thought you knew—"

"Knew what?"

"Well, the men...I mean, Larry has talked to the other firefighters who were on the job when Ray was—" She pursed her lips and color flooded her perfect cheeks. "There's talk, is all I'm saying."

Janice's throat filled with bile, and she gritted her teeth. "What kind of talk?"

"That, well, maybe Logan—as fine a firefighter as he is, I'm sure—feels responsible for Ray—"

"Are you saying Logan killed my husband?"

"Oh, no, that's not what I mean. It's just that Larry says Logan has been different since the accident. Not so, uh, friendly, I guess. Like he feels guilty."

"There's no reason for him to. I'm sure he did everything he could to save Ray."

"I'm sure you're right. Larry probably misunderstood." Andrea pushed away from the counter. "I really must get back to my baseboards. Such tedious work, but someone has to do it." She smiled brightly, then hustled from the kitchen, tossing an absent "Thank you for the water" over her shoulder.

Stunned, Janice stood in her wake. She didn't want Logan blaming himself for what had happened. Didn't want to think there was nothing between them—not even friendship—except for his need to atone for something that couldn't be helped.

Blaming the vagrants who started the fire in the abandoned warehouse was far more appropriate. Or more likely, the fault lay with poverty and indigents who had simply been trying to heat a can of beans. The plan had gone deadly wrong.

But could Logan have made a mistake on the roof that day? a niggling voice asked, and could that be the reason he'd been so helpful to her? Could he really have that much cause to feel guilty? What would that say about the budding feelings she had for him? What would that say about her own disloyalty to her husband, unfaithful though he had been?

The back door clattered open, and Janice started, half expecting to see the ghost of her husband accusing her of betraying his memory with the man who had killed him.

Instead of a ghost, in walked Kimberly Lydell— now Mrs. Jay Tolliver, Janice mentally corrected— carrying two big grocery sacks.

"What's all that?" Janice asked, relieved to see a flesh-and-blood human instead of the specter of her guilty conscience.

"Lunch. I was assigned kitchen duty, which probably says something about my skills as a painter."

Smiling, the one-time TV news anchor put the sacks on the kitchen counter. Last spring, during an earthquake, she'd been scarred by falling debris. Since then she'd become the host of a late-night, call-in talk show on local public radio, a popular program with firefighters and insomniacs in Paseo del Real. Janice had been known to listen on nights when she'd been unable to sleep. The topics were wide-ranging and often fascinating.

"You didn't have to do that," Janice said. "I was going to make up some chicken-pasta salad—"

"Save yours for your family. I already raided the deli at the grocery store for salads and fried chicken legs, plus I picked up the makings for sandwiches. I thought everyone could do their own lunch whenever they got hungry." Kim dipped into the first sack, brought out a big container of potato salad. "Picnic à la painting party."

Janice found a package of paper plates, napkins and some plastic utensils in the other sack along with canned cold drinks. "Everyone's being so kind." Tears suddenly pressed at the back of her eyes, from guilt and shame and confusion. "It's…it's embarrassing to have to ask for so much help. I don't know how I'll ever repay—"

"Shh, there's no need to repay anyone." Kim gave her a quick hug. "You'd do the same for us, wouldn't you?"

"Yes, but—"

"No buts, either. Losing Ray was a terrible tragedy for all of us, especially the men who were his friends.

Doing this helps everyone to deal with their grief.'' In a casual gesture, she tucked a few strands of her collar-length blond hair behind her ear. ''Now then, we're going to need some serving spoons—''

''I'll get them.'' The serving utensils were in a drawer beside the sink. Trying to keep her troubling thoughts in check, Janice made a selection while Kim put the makings for lunch out on the kitchen table.

''It's too bad you're going to have to sell the house,'' Kim said. ''I know it would be easier for you and the children if you didn't have to make so many changes all at once.''

''I'm afraid that's not one of my options.''

''Are you going to stay in Paseo?''

''I plan to, assuming I can find a job.''

Kim glanced up from her task of ripping open the napkin package. ''What kind of work do you do?''

''You mean besides scrub floors and wash kids' clothes?'' She gave a self-deprecating laugh. ''The last time I earned a paycheck I was in college making sandwiches in the student union.''

''What was your major?''

''History, but I didn't come close to graduating, not that there are many jobs around for historians who do have a bachelor's degree. Liking to rummage around in old, yellowed books for arcane facts isn't listed as a job title in the want ads. I thought I'd try to brush up on my typing. We bought the kids a computer last year, so I can study up on word-processing pro-grams.'' She pried the lid off the potato salad and stuck in a spoon. "What I'm saying is that I'm not terribly employable, which scares me to death."

"You're a smart woman. You'll find something."

"I certainly hope so." She'd have to find it soon, too. Every mail delivery seemed to bring another overdue bill. Whatever had Ray been thinking? Assuming he'd been thinking with his brain at all instead of another part of his anatomy.

A wave of shame washed over her, not because of Ray's adultery, but because she'd allowed him to steal her self-esteem. She'd *believed* him when he'd said she didn't have a head for numbers. Well, she was doing the addition now and the picture was bleak because of Ray's shortcomings. Not hers.

Somehow she and the children would be fine without him. She *believed* that now. She had to.

When the food was set out on the table, Kim circulated through the house to let the workers know lunch was ready. Janice went outside to tell the men they could come eat whenever they wanted to take a break.

The men were laughing and wisecracking out front, making disparaging comments about the skill—or lack thereof—of their fellow firefighters.

"I don't know, Tolliver," Mike Gables said to his buddy Jay. "You've got more paint on yourself than you have on the house. You sure you aren't still having some problems with your eyesight?"

"I can see you waving that brush around, but it doesn't look like you know where to put it," Jay retorted. "The speed you're working, we're gonna be here a month."

"According to my wife, it's not speed that counts. She prefers slow and leisurely. But you wouldn't know about—"

"Yeah, well, Kim says—"

"Gentlemen," Janice interrupted, grinning at their bantering. "Anytime you want to take a break from comparing your styles, lunch is ready in the kitchen."

Jay looked down from his perch on the ladder. "We'll be right there, just as soon as Gables figures out how to get it right."

"Yeah, like you know, huh? How many houses have you painted?"

Janice left them to their good-natured bickering, circling the house to tell the others about lunch. Above the chatter of conversation, she could hear Greg Turrick crooning a country-western tune, a pleasant accompaniment to the mundane task of painting.

Reaching the rear of the house, she winced at the sight of Kevin standing on a ladder and stretching to his full reach to dab a bit of paint on the far corner of a windowsill. She held her breath until he righted himself.

"Lunchtime, Kevin," she called.

"In a minute, Mom." He dipped his brush in the paint can again. "I gotta finish this first."

Every overly protective instinct rose up in her. She wanted to pull Kevin down off the ladder. Cuddle him. Protect him from all risk of injury. But she knew he was learning to be a man here among these firefighters. She wouldn't deprive him of that chance.

With her heart in her throat and a prayer on her lips, she turned away. At least she didn't have to watch.

Spotting Maddie playing with Buttons at the back of the yard, she smiled to herself. She should have known. If a dog, or any animal, was within two blocks, that's where she'd find her daughter.

Then and there, she promised herself she'd talk to Mike Gables about the puppies Buttons had sired. Her daughter deserved to have something special of her own to love.

So did she, Janice mused, the image of Logan popping effortlessly into her imagination. She chided herself for her wayward thoughts, particularly after what Andrea had told her. Guilt was not a good basis on which to form a relationship.

"Honey, lunch is ready in the kitchen," she told her daughter. "You go on inside, and I'll be there in a minute to help you."

"Can I give Buttons some lunch, too? He's hungry. I know he is."

Janice doubted that. The dalmatian looked trim but well fed. "*One* piece of lunch meat," she conceded, "*after* you eat your own sandwich."

Popping up like a jack-in-the-box, Maddie went racing toward the house. Janice suspected her daughter would wolf down her own sandwich in order to return to her beloved Buttons as quickly as possible.

Continuing on her tour of the house—and noting with pleasure the improvements that had already been made—she found Logan working alone on the far side of the house. He seemed very intense, his concentration absolute. She imagined he did everything that way, giving whatever task he had at hand his full attention.

Including making love.

That thought had been hovering for days just outside her awareness. Once again the sting of guilt assailed her. Only minutes ago she'd been told Logan felt guilty about her husband's death. If that were true, even considering making love with him was the ultimate betrayal of her husband.

A husband who had betrayed her with another woman.

Dear heaven, at some primal level did she simply want to get even?

"Hi, Jan, did you want something?" Logan asked. He lifted the Giants' baseball cap he was wearing and threaded his fingers through his sweat-dampened hair.

She snapped out of her trance. Oh, yes, she wanted a lot of things but not this sense of confusion, this inability to evaluate her emotions rationally. Her world kept tipping, spinning out of control in ways she'd never before imagined.

"Are you here because you blame yourself for Ray's death?" she blurted.

Slowly, Logan descended the ladder. What had given him away? What gesture? What slip of the tongue? "I was up there with him," he said cautiously. "On the roof."

"I don't believe you were to blame. It was an accident. Wasn't it?"

She studied him with guileless eyes, eyes that were trying to read his thoughts. He willed her not to ask for the details of that fateful day. How could he possibly tell her, or anyone else, the truth?

He had the urge to reach out to her, pull her into his arms, tell her there were some things she wasn't meant to know. That it didn't matter how or why her husband had died. But he couldn't do that. She'd once loved Ray enough to marry him. Even though her husband had been unfaithful, that didn't give Logan the right to rub salt in the wound. Or risk destroying her kids' memories of their father.

It didn't matter if she blamed him or not. Not when he blamed himself.

Opening her mouth, she started to speak, then apparently thought better of whatever she'd been about to say. "Lunch is ready whenever you are. In the kitchen."

Tension eased from his shoulders. "Fine. Just let me finish up this little bit of trim." He gestured toward the spot he'd been working. "I'll be there in a minute."

She seemed to want to stay, to ask the question that had been so obviously on the tip of her tongue. Logan didn't want her to.

Turning, paintbrush in hand, he climbed back up the ladder. Below him he could sense her confusion, her fear that if someone other than Logan had been on that roof, Ray might still be alive.

Damn it! That's what he was afraid of, too. It twisted in his gut night and day. Somehow he should have stopped Ray from even going up on that roof. It would have been better if Logan had risked it alone.

LOGAN CAME OUT of the civil-service testing room the following week, his head pounding with facts and figures, procedures for safely maneuvering a fire truck through the streets of Paseo. He checked his watch. He'd warned Janice he'd likely be late for soccer practice. He'd been right.

He grinned like a little kid—from relief that the test was over and because he'd be seeing Janice within minutes.

Only a few cars were in the school parking lot, teachers working late and Janice's familiar van. She needed a newer vehicle, something with air bags and a lower profile that wasn't at risk in high winds.

He'd caught himself worrying about her a lot lately, and more than just about her strained finances. He worried about what she'd do if her car broke down, who she would call. What if her plumbing backed up? Did she know a reliable plumber or would some jerk take advantage of her, overcharging her because she was a woman alone?

It wasn't his business to worry about her. But he did. He couldn't seem to help himself.

Maddie spotted him from across the schoolyard. She raced toward him, and he scooped her up in his arms, loving her big, welcoming smile and inhaling her sweaty scent.

"Hey, sprite, what's happening?"

"Mommy says when we move to a new house, I can have one of Buttons's babies."

"So, you wore her down, huh?" He kept walking toward the soccer field, listening to Maddie chatter, but he only had eyes for Janice, who was surrounded by nine-year-old boys. She made quite an attractive package, looking youthful and trim in her shorts and tank top. If the boys had been a few years older, Logan would have been jealous of the attention she was giving them.

"Uh-uh. She said she wanted one, too."

"You're going to have *two* puppies?" He feigned amazement.

The child giggled, a high-pitched, happy sound. "No, silly, we're gonna share *one* puppy."

"Ah. Now I understand." Lowering her to the ground, he gave her a wink and patted her head. "I gotta get to work or your mom will fire me as assistant coach."

"Uh-uh. She likes you."

Did she? Logan couldn't be sure. No question, she was grateful for his help. But gratitude wasn't what he was looking for—not that he had a right to ask for anything more. Besides, since the weekend painting party, she'd been hesitant around him, as if his sense of guilt was as infectious as a flu virus.

He reached the middle of the field as the boys separated into scrimmage teams.

"Sorry I'm late," he said.

"How'd the test go?"

"Long and tiring, but I think I did okay."

Her smile was the mirror image of her daughter's, and had a similarly profound effect on his heart, but in a more adult way.

"I'm sure you did better than okay."

"We'll know the results in a week."

She glanced toward the players. "You're not playing dodge ball, Terry. Use your feet. Help Kevin protect the goal. You're the last line of defense before the goalie, and he can't do it all on his own."

"You're getting good at this."

"I'm faking it, but don't tell the boys." Laughing, she kept her eyes on the ragged soccer play, throwing in a little body language when a kicked ball just eased past the goalie. "Nice try, Chuck. Good effort, Kevin. Let's take the ball back to the midline and try again."

She glanced up at Logan. "I listed the house with a Realtor today. He says the market is really good right now, he even thinks he's got a buyer who's transferring to Paseo and had a deal go sour at the last minute on a house in our same tract when the owners backed out. The family is scheduled to show up in a couple of weeks. The Realtor thinks I ought to go ahead now and have the house tented for termites." She reached out with her foot to stop an errant pass, then kicked the ball back into the field of play. "Which means the kids and I will have to stay overnight in a hotel unless I can con a neighbor into letting us move in with them."

"Move in with me, instead." The impulsive words

were out before he stopped to think through all the ramifications of his invitation.

Her head snapped around. "We couldn't impose on you—"

"It's no imposition. The kids would have to double up in the extra bedroom. You can have my bed, and I'll sleep on the couch."

"But you've already done so much. I'm sure Debbie down the street—the family with the swimming pool—wouldn't mind us camping out—"

"We're only talking about one night. The kids could fish right from the dock at my front door or they could swim—"

"You live on a lake?"

"Lake Almador. It's really a reservoir and not all that big. But there are a few cabins along the north shore, most of them used only for weekends, and the lake is stocked with ten-inchers. Midweek, particularly during the winter, it feels pretty remote from the world."

She got a dreamy look in her eyes. "Sounds like heaven."

"Not quite that good, but as close as I could find within commuting distance of my job. I'll check my work schedule. We'll do it when I've got a couple of days off in a row."

"There's a teachers' institute coming up at school. The children would have that day off, too. We'll have to work it around the soccer schedule."

"No problem. We'll plan to do it when the kids are off from school. It'll be like—" He came close to saying *like a honeymoon.* That was an odd thought. You didn't take two kids on a honeymoon. And getting married was a prerequisite to that kind of a trip. He didn't dare read anything more into her hopeful expression than a desire to get away for a couple of days. "We'll make it into a mini-vacation."

He'd concentrate like hell on being a good host, which meant he'd have to keep his hands off Janice.

Looking at the sparkle in her ginger-brown eyes and the way her sensual lips curved into a smile, he knew that wasn't going to be easy.

Chapter Seven

The fire tone sounded.

"Engines 61 and 62," Emma Jean's voice blared throughout the station house. "Car fire on the south-bound off-ramp, Highway 99 and First Street."

Logan stepped to the side of the bay as the men of the two engine companies raced to their vehicles. The ladder truck wouldn't be rolling on this one—no roofs to ventilate, no ladders to climb to attempt a rescue. The surge of adrenaline that had pumped through Logan's veins ebbed. His turn would come another time.

As the engines rolled out onto the street, sirens wailing, the station quieted almost as if the building itself was taking a deep breath. The air, which had been filled with the vitality of more than a dozen men laughing and talking, stilled, subtly replaced by a hint of anxiety. Even a car fire could be dangerous. Fire-fighters were out of the station risking their lives.

Logan imagined Janice must cringe every time she heard a siren. She'd lost one husband to the red devil. It didn't make any sense that she'd ever take that risk again. A man would be a fool to hope that she would.

Sliding his hands into the pockets of his uniform trousers, Logan strolled out back to where Big Red was parked. A pair of holey tennis shoes filled with sockless feet stuck out from beneath the ancient fire truck.

"Hey, Tommy, how's it going?" Logan peered down through the open engine compartment at the adolescent working below.

"Just about got this transmission nailed. A couple of more hours and we'll give it a smoke test."

"It'd be embarrassing if we had a fire here at the station."

"Well, yeah, you know what I mean." The boy gave himself a shove and rolled out from under the truck on a crawler. His blue coveralls were spotted with grease stains.

"You're a marvel, Tommy. I wouldn't even know how to begin to remake a transmission."

Standing, the boy pulled a rag from his hip pocket and wiped his hands. "It's no big deal." The acne on his face turned an even brighter shade of red than usual.

"So Big Red's going to be ready for the parade?"

"I guess. Unless something else busts."

Which was entirely possible, given the age of the old truck. Still, they'd had it painted and it sparkled in the sunlight. It'd be a real hit in the parade.

"Can I asked you something, Logan?"

"Sure." Tommy's parents were divorced, and Logan sensed the boy's father wasn't around much. The men of Station Six had de facto adopted the kid as their joint little brother.

"Am I really going to get to ride on Big Red in the parade?"

"Of course. Nobody has earned the ride more than you."

Stuffing the rag back in his pocket, the boy studied the holey tip of his shoe, digging it into the asphalt. "I heard some of the guys talking. You know, they were, like, saying they were gonna bring girls—wives and stuff."

Ah, now he knew where this conversation was headed. "You got somebody you want to bring?"

Without lifting his head, the boy shrugged. "I guess."

"Has she got a name?"

"Uh, Rachel. Her ol' man's got a great muscle car. Totally out of sight!"

Logan suppressed a smile. "Go ahead and ask her. I'm sure it'll be fine."

"Yeah, maybe I will." He glanced up at Logan. "You gonna bring your girl?"

The boy's question stopped him. He didn't have a girl, which hadn't stopped the image of Janice sitting next to him while he drove Big Red down the parade route from popping into his head. Or the sound of crowds cheering. Flags waving. Her proud smile meant just for him.

Wasn't going to happen.

He hadn't done much of the restoration work, mostly scraping away the rust and polishing the metal to a smooth gloss. The guys who had done the most mechanical repairs would get preference to ride the truck in the parade. But maybe he could suggest that Janice, the widow of a firefighter, and her children, could be given the honor of riding. She might like that. Certainly her kids would.

"I don't have a girl," he finally said to Tommy.

"Maybe you will by then?"

Less than a month from now? Logan didn't think so, particularly since the only woman he'd been thinking about lately was Janice. For him, she was the one woman who was totally off limits.

"It's not real likely," he finally said.

Pulling the rag from his back pocket, Tommy wiped at an invisible spot on the fender. "Did you know Mike Gables wants to send a fire truck to some folks he knows in Kosovo?"

"Not Big Red, I hope."

The boy shrugged. "He says it would be too expensive to ship it."

"Not to mention the rest of the guys would hand him his head if he did anything with Big Red after all their work."

"Well, yeah, I guess. But he says this little village he's talking about practically got wiped out in the war. They could sure use a fire truck, even an old one like this."

Logan closed his hand over the boy's shoulder. "I don't think you have anything to worry about. Big Red will be the star of the parade. Gables isn't going to ship it anywhere."

"But afterwards?"

"I don't think—"

"It wouldn't be so bad, thinking about folks you've never seen getting a truck like this and being able to put out their fires when they don't have anything better."

"Put like that?" Logan smiled at the boy, who appeared to have a generous heart to go with his mechanical talents. "No, it might not be so bad. But for now, why don't we just concentrate on getting the ol' crate running good enough to make it all the way down the parade route."

Tommy returned his grin. "Better not let her hear you call her a crate. The ol' girl has feelings, you know."

With a laugh, Logan gave the boy an affectionate pat on the back. Every man at Station Six would just be happy if Big Red didn't break down in the parade. Any thoughts of what would happen to the truck after that would be someone else's problem, not Logan's.

JANICE DROPPED the last of the boxes of cereal into a black plastic garbage sack and tied the neck shut to keep the contents safe from the fumigation fumes. As the Realtor had predicted, she'd already accepted an offer on the house. Her head spun with everything that needed to be done in order to move out in two weeks, which is what the new buyers had demanded in trade for the full asking price.

But for now, she could only think of her two days at Logan's house. She'd barely been able to sleep last night. That was foolish, she knew. He was only being kind. There was no reason her heart should beat double time at the thought of sleeping in his bed, not when he'd be sleeping on the couch.

She sighed and picked up the sack. Except for one soccer practice, she hadn't seen him in the past week. His work schedule had kept him away.

"Kevin, have you got your suitcase ready?" she called. "The termite men will be here any minute."

"Coming!"

"Maddie! You too!"

Her daughter came into the kitchen dragging a small suitcase on wheels behind her, a stuffed giraffe under her arm. "Can I take Bruce with me?"

"Of course, honey. Take him out to the car, will you?" Janice was quite sure there were two more stuffed animals in her suitcase, barely leaving enough room for a change of clothes. But for one night, she wouldn't need much.

As Maddie went out the back door, Janice's neighbor Debbie Longacre appeared.

"Hey, hon, Jimmy told me this morning you're getting your house tented."

"For termites, right."

"Well, where are you going to stay? You're not moving to a motel or anything like that, are you? You know you'd be welcome at our place. I was going to have the kids over for a swim this afternoon, anyway. The boys could double up—"

"Oh, thanks, Debbie, but we're staying with a friend."

Her dark eyebrows lifted. On the overweight side, Debbie had a quick smile, a generous heart and a good ear for anything worthy of gossip. "A friend?"

"One of the firefighters Ray worked with."

"And his wife?"

Turning away, Janice went to the cupboard that held crackers, bread and other snacks, and started dropping them into a garbage bag. "He's not married."

"Really?" Debbie asked, her inflection rising suggestively. "Is there something happening you haven't told me?"

"He's been a good friend since Ray died, that's all there is to it." Which wasn't to say Janice hadn't considered other possibilities—all of which she'd rejected. "He lives out on Lake Almador, and he thought the kids would enjoy fishing off his dock."

"Uh-huh. Bet that's why your ears are turning red. Just a friend, huh?"

Filled with embarrassment, she whirled far too abruptly, forcing her friend to take a step back. "Debbie, I appreciate your offer to let us stay with you, but I've got it covered, okay?"

"And I'm butting in."

She was, of course, but Janice didn't want to hurt her friend's feelings. "No, it's not that—"

"You just be careful, you hear? A woman as recently widowed as you…. Well, I had a friend in your same fix and she made some pretty bad mistakes before she got her act back together. I wouldn't want—"

"I'm giving my children a chance to go fishing. Nothing more than that."

"If you say so." Debbie didn't look convinced, but she gave Janice a quick hug anyway.

Janice wasn't convinced either. But that was her story and she was going to stick with it—even if it killed her. She was *not* going to make Logan responsible for fulfilling the fantasies her active imagination had conjured up in recent days. And nights. She had no right even to be looking at a man, much less day dreaming about him. It wasn't fair to Logan.

She certainly shouldn't burden him with Ray's debts or her problems, any more than she already had.

Instead she should be pursuing her independence, which she was, although the classifieds offered scant hope for any well-paying jobs for which she had the necessary qualifications. Still, she'd made appointments next week at two temporary employment agencies. It would be a beginning.

At the same time, she'd have to start a vigorous search for someplace where she and her children could live. Someplace she could afford.

Kevin popped into the kitchen. "Mom, didn't Dad have a fishing pole someplace? I looked in the front closet, and all I could find was his baseball glove."

"He wasn't much of a fisherman, honey."

"He went out on the boat with Mike Gables once."

"I think they were scuba diving." Or more likely, sitting around drinking beer and bragging.

Debbie said, "I think my Fred has a pole, if you want to borrow it."

"It's all right." She looped her arm around Kevin's

shoulders. "I'm sure Logan has extra poles and lures, or whatever you'll need."

Debbie gave her that suggestive eyebrow look again. "You just be sure he doesn't go trolling where it'll get you into deep water, you hear?"

"I'll be careful," Janice said.

After Debbie had left, Kevin said, "What was Debbie talking about, Mom? Deep water?"

"Just a reminder to wear life vests if we go out in Logan's boat." She turned her son around, giving him a little shove toward his bedroom. "Get your suitcase out to the car, honey. It's almost eight o'clock. The termite men will be here any minute."

With a troubled sigh, she dropped the rest of the snacks into the sack. She wished Debbie's advice wasn't quite so wise—or so right on track. She needed to be careful not to get in over her depth.

In the grand scheme of things, staying at a friend's house for one night held no significance at all. She'd do well to remember that.

LOGAN PACED the narrow dirt road behind his house. After months without rain, the dust was powdery fine, the pine trees that shaded the place coated light beige. Except where a winter creek ran on the opposite side of the road, the scant covering of spring grass had dried and withered with the summer heat. A late-season butterfly searched for a place to light. Out on the lake, the sound of children's laughter drifted on the still morning air.

He'd given Janice directions to his place, but the turnoff could be tricky to spot.

Maybe he should have picked them up and driven them here himself.

Maybe he shouldn't have invited them at all. Having Janice in his house—sleeping in his bed—felt too intimate. Too tempting. Too much of a strain on his too-active libido.

Shading his eyes with his hand, he turned toward the sound of an approaching vehicle. The minivan appeared at the turn of the road, trailed by a billowing rooster tail of dust. Janice stopped the car and the side door sprang open, Kevin and Maddie bursting out.

The five-year-old ran right into his arms. "Hi, Logan! We gets to be fishermens!"

"That's right, sprite."

The boy lingered back, playing it cool.

Logan gave the youngster a wink and watched as a slow smile curved the boy's lips.

As if that tentative smile were worth a million bucks, Logan's heart filled with a combination of pleasure and regret. These weren't his children, their mother not his wife. They weren't his family. He could only offer them a temporary sanctuary.

Janice eased out of the van more slowly than her children had exited the car. Her palms were wet, leaving a damp print on the door handle. Fluttery wings of butterflies teased through her stomach. Staying with Debbie would have been a much safer choice. But she'd played it safe all of her life—with the exception of when Ray had swept her off her feet.

Wiping her hands on the seat of her shorts, she rounded the corner of the van. Maddie had already claimed Logan, tugging him toward the house.

"Welcome to Stronghold." His gaze met hers, the corners of his eyes crinkling as he smiled, and the butterflies turned into sparrows.

"Stronghold?" she asked.

He gestured toward the house, a modern, one-story log cabin that nestled among lodgepole pines and clusters of red-bark manzanita bushes. The word *Stronghold* was etched into a rustic wooden sign that hung above the steps to the front porch.

"Very nice." She smiled, thinking Logan's home looked like a safe haven from the pressures of the world. "Do invaders attack your castle often?"

"Outside of family members, today's the first time."

Pleasurable warmth seeped through her at what she took to be his admission that she was the first woman to visit his hideaway.

Maddie tugged on Logan's hand. "Come on, Mommy," she said over her shoulder. "Logan's gonna take us fishing."

"Let's get the suitcases first, young lady. You, too, Kevin." Her son had already walked past the house to get a view of the lake beyond.

He came running back. "I saw his boat, Mom." He whirled toward Logan. "Can we go out on the boat, Logan? Can we?"

"If you're willing to row."

Kevin's expression crumbled. "You don't have a motor?"

"The lake's too small, motors aren't allowed. No speedboats, water skiers, Jet Skis. It's one of the lake's charms."

Kevin scowled, and Janice ruffled his short hair, a darker shade than Logan's sandy-brown but just as straight. "Think of all the muscles you'll get rowing the boat."

"A motor would be cooler," he grumbled.

Logan laughed, a delighted sound that seemed to bounce off the trees, inviting others to join in the fun. As if by magic, the crease that so intrigued Janice appeared in his cheek and squint lines fanned out from his hazel eyes. Janice's heart stuttered. This man was so potent, yet she didn't think he realized how he affected her. She didn't dare be the one to tell him.

Disconnecting his hand from Maddie's, he reached into the van, pulling out the smaller suitcases and handing them off to the children. Then he got Janice's overnight case.

"Let me show you where you'll be sleeping. Then we can go for a boat ride. Later this evening the fishing will be better."

They all followed him into the house.

It was cozy and inviting: a big, native-rock fireplace sandwiched between pine bookshelves filled one wall of the living room, and a picture window looked out over the lake. Following an open-floor plan, the dining area flowed into a small but efficient kitchen with yet another view of the lake. Not a thing was out of place, the counters were clear except for a coffeemaker. Wood tables gleamed, and the air held the scent of lemon as though Logan had spent the morning polishing everything in sight.

"This isn't like any bachelor pad I've ever heard about," Janice commented. The stress of day-to-day coping with life eased from her shoulders and neck only to be replaced with a different kind of tension lower in her body. A pleasant sensation she'd almost forgotten during the recent years of her marriage.

He cocked a brow. "You've visited a lot of bachelor pads, have you?"

"I said *heard* about—I read widely."

"Ah." He nodded, a spark of masculine mischief in his eyes.

"I found my room!" Maddie cried from the side of the house away from the lake, disturbing the sexual sizzle that had curled Janice's toes.

"Do I have to sleep with her?" Kevin complained.

"One night won't hurt you," Janice insisted, not fully confident Logan was feeling the same sensual pull. "It's separate beds."

"What if she snores?"

"Gee, honey, last time I checked, a train going through your bedroom wouldn't wake you. I don't think Maddie snoring will be a problem."

He didn't look convinced.

While the children argued over who got which bed, Logan showed Janice to his room. Her gaze collided with the giant king-size bed nearly filling the room, large enough that she and the children could all sleep together without bothering each other.

Or she and Logan could indulge in other activities there.

Her mouth going dry at the thought, she quickly glanced away, only to see him in the mirror smiling at her, a heated look in his eyes. Surely he wasn't reading her thoughts. Or entertaining the same erotic possibilities.

"I put out clean towels in the bathroom," he said. "If you need anything else, just let me know."

She had an urge to tell him exactly what she needed, but that would be beyond foolish.

"I hate putting you out of your own bed. Why don't I sleep on the couch and you can—"

"I'll be fine. I promise."

Leaning against the doorjamb, he seemed to fill all the available space. Such a tall man needed plenty of room to sleep, but he was willing to sacrifice his comfort for hers. Janice wondered when was the last time Ray had been as thoughtful.

Maybe never.

With a shake of her head, she chided herself for thinking like that. She didn't dare fall into the trap of comparing everything Logan did to Ray's failings. No man was perfect. Before she could even consider a new relationship, she had to prove to herself that she could stand on her own two feet.

"So?" she said, mentally stiffening her resolve. "Where's this fancy boat of yours?"

HE'D FIXED a picnic lunch for them. That had been easy. Getting to the island in the middle of the lake to eat the lunch was a different matter.

Logan sat in the stern of the boat grinning like a fool as Kevin and Maddie, each working a separate oar, valiantly tried to row in a straight line. He lifted his ball cap and ran his fingers through his hair. Things weren't going well in the rowing department. About ten feet off shore, they'd been going in circles for the past five minutes.

"She's doing it wrong," Kevin complained.

"Rowing requires cooperation," Logan pointed out mildly.

"But she's too little."

"Uh-uh." Maddie's oar spanked the water, sending a cascade of drops over Janice, who was sitting in the bow.

Holding her straw hat on her head, Janice shot him an amused look. "Are you sure we aren't still tied to the dock?"

Logan feigned surprise. "I thought you untied the lines."

Halting his stroke in mid-air, Kevin cried, "Hey, no way! I'm not gonna—"

"It's okay, son," Logan said. Kneeling, he placed his hands around Maddie's waist and lifted her, backing up again so she was sitting between his legs facing her brother. "Here we go. Kevin, you grab both oars and Maddie will, too. The three of us will get this thing going."

"I could do it—"

"I know, but your mom and I are getting hungry."

Operating this way was a little awkward, but the boat began moving slowly toward the island. The sun was high in the sky; only the faintest breeze riffled the water. Logan felt as good and carefree as he could remember feeling. Except it was a moment stolen out of time. Not his to hold. Whether he deserved it or not, Ray should be the one here with his children.

With his wife.

Logan's guilty conscience slammed into him with the force of a fire ax. Could he have hesitated to act that fateful morning because he envied Ray? Because at some level he'd been afraid to admit, he wanted Janice for himself?

Hell of a thing to think about now.

He tried to recall that morning. His irritation with Ray for being late, his disgust that he was so wiped out he moved at a snail's pace. His assessment of the fire as they threw a thirty-five-foot ladder against the wall and started up.

He didn't remember thinking about Janice. He should have. Maybe she wouldn't be a widow now.

HOURS LATER, with the sun setting, when Kevin and Maddie caught their very first fish off the end of his dock, Logan was still feeling guilty. He told himself it was a stupid reaction. Ray never would have taken his kids fishing. That wasn't his thing.

His loss, Logan thought as he looked at the grin on Maddie's face.

"How 'bout I clean these fish for you and cook 'em up for breakfast?" he asked.

"We have to *eat* them?" Maddie said with a gasp, tears flooding her eyes. "I wanted to *keep* mine forever 'n ever! Like my goldfish!"

"You dork." Despite the derogatory name for his sister, Kevin set his fishing pole aside long enough to awkwardly pat her on the shoulder. "Your goldfish bowl isn't big enough for these guys. And if you kept 'em, they'd just begin to stink."

These guys were barely eight inches long, hardly big enough to make a meal.

Sitting in a folding chair on the dock, Janice smiled at her children. "I think it would be wonderful if Logan cooked us trout for breakfast. I can remember my daddy catching catfish and my mama fixing it in a batter. It's really good."

"Trout's better rolled in cornmeal and fried in butter." Fortunately, Logan had planned ahead. He had a couple of fair-size trout he'd bought at the meat market in town he'd fry up with these smaller ones. Lake Almador rarely provided a big enough catch to make a meal, even for one. It was more like pond fishing for the kids.

Maddie seemed mollified, for the moment, Kevin content to be his sister's hero.

Feeling relaxed, Janice watched the sun sink below the coastal range of mountains, tingeing the clouds pink. The lake had gone from blue to black, lights coming on in the cabins along the northern shoreline. Across the way, campfires flickered among the trees.

Closer at hand, miniature waves whispered against the gravel beach, like the gentle stroke of a man's hand caressing a woman. Arousing her.

Forcefully, she pressed the thought aside.

"So when does the bagpipe concert begin?" she asked.

Logan chuckled. "You must be trying to frighten the rest of the fish away."

"You did promise me a jig."

"Hmm, that I did."

"You play those awful bagpipes?" Kevin asked. "Yuck. They sound worse than fingernails on the blackboard."

"Now there's a challenge if I ever heard one. It seems it's fallen to me to teach you folks the finer nuances of pipe playing."

Kevin groaned.

Maddie said, "Can I squeeze the bag?"

"We'll see," he hedged. Agilely, he rose to his feet and walked back to the house, carrying his empty coffee cup.

He was gone so long, Janice began to wonder if he'd changed his mind about playing the pipes for them. Or if he'd gotten an emergency call to report for duty, perhaps a wildfire had broken out somewhere.

About the time the children had totally lost interest in fishing, he reappeared—wearing his kilt, knee-high socks sporting tassels, and black, shiny shoes.

Yep, she mused. Even in the twilight his legs were solid tens.

He struck a pose in the middle of the dock, slid the bag under his left arm and tucked the blowpipe into the corner of his lips. His foot started to tap and the pads of his fingertips flew over the chanter holes, creating a lively tune.

Maddie was the first one up, dancing in rhythm to the music. Janice couldn't resist, either, dragging Kevin to his feet. Laughing and holding hands, the three of them circled Logan. All they lacked were white robes to make them look like druids performing an ancient ritual.

Logan segued into another tune. He kept playing until Janice was breathless, unable to take another step. She gasped for air while the children still danced. Eventually even their energy was spent.

Reaching the end of the song, Logan let the remaining air escape from the bag in a low wheeze. From somewhere down the lake, scattered applause broke out.

"Do you suppose they're clapping because I finally quit playing?" he asked dryly.

"I'm sure it's because they thought you were wonderful."

"Play some more," Maddie urged.

"Yeah, play a march or somethin'," Kevin suggested.

She hooked her arms over her children's shoulders. "That's enough for tonight. Bedtime, guys."

"Aw, Mom," they chorused.

Logan volunteered to dismantle the fishing poles and take care of the day's catch, such as it was, and wished the kids goodnight. Meanwhile, Janice ushered her children inside to oversee their bedtime rituals.

By the time she returned, Logan was playing a haunting melody on the bagpipes. She didn't recognize the tune but the theme was obvious in the lingering notes, the depth of emotion apparent in the mood he created. Lost love. She felt every lonely beat of the music in her own heart, the discordant minor notes that left her aching.

Sensing her presence, he ended the song. The music lingered in the air like a sweet perfume, yet somehow melancholy.

"The kids down for the count?"

"Yes." She stopped on the dock near him. The moon had risen, a golden half circle that cast a shimmering path of light on the still water of the lake. "That was a beautiful song. The whole day was beautiful. Just perfect."

"I'm glad you enjoyed yourself." His voice was low. Husky. Intimate.

"Thank you," she whispered, her throat tight with emotion.

Standing on tiptoe, she meant to give him a quick kiss on his cheek. Instead, he turned and captured her lips with his own. His hand cupped the back of her head, drawing her closer.

She melted into him, into his kiss. Her lips parted. With a swift penetration, he expertly took advantage of the opportunity. She tasted the coffee he'd been sipping and a special flavor that seemed uniquely his own.

In the absence of the bagpipes playing, crickets had taken up his song, lonely and searching for a mate.

Janice felt herself surrendering to all that longing—his and hers. Her hands rested on his broad chest, her right elbow brushing the velvet-covered bag tucked beneath his arm, her fingers digging into the fine woolen sash that angled from shoulder to waist, wanting to get closer. Wanting the intimacy that had been denied her so long, wanting what she hadn't realized she'd been missing.

He deepened the kiss as if he understood.

Lost in a sensual haze, she made a soft, aching sound at the back of her throat.

That's when he broke the kiss and backed away.

The loss of contact made her want to weep.

Chapter Eight

"I shouldn't have done that." In the moonlight, Janice's eyes were luminous, and Logan cursed himself for coming so close to losing control. For forgetting he was responsible for her husband's death.

The tip of her tongue swept out to lick her lips. To taste him again? he wondered. Or to wipe away the evidence of his kiss? Either way he felt the gesture right behind the black leather sporran slung between his hips, an official part of his highland costume.

"Please don't apologize. You didn't do anything wrong."

He wanted to do something very wrong. He wanted to kiss her until they were both senseless with need. Wanted to take her inside, lie her down on his bed and kiss every inch of her. Make slow, lingering love with her while her kids slept only a room away.

He couldn't do that. He had no right. It had taken all of his willpower—it was still taking every ounce of his strength—not to act on the ache that filled his loins.

"You tempt me, Janice." His voice was thick in his

throat. "You tempt me with the way your lips curl into a smile, with your quiet forbearance, your gentle way with your children. I have no right to give into that temptation. No right at all."

"And if I gave you that right?" Her barely audible voice trembled in the same way a pebble ripples the surface of a lake on a windless day.

Unable to help himself, he touched her cheek with his fingertips. Creamy skin flushed with the heat of wanting. Her whole body would feel that way, warm and wanting, pliable beneath his hands. "That would be a gift I couldn't accept no matter how much I might want to. Not now."

"You mean because Ray hasn't been dead long?"

"You're vulnerable. I don't want to take advantage of you." And Logan's own feelings of guilt—justified or not—were too great a burden for her delicate shoulders to bear.

She exhaled a tiny sigh. "You and my neighbor seem to think I'll do something rash, as if being widowed is to be suddenly let out of a bottle, sure to do something foolish."

"Would you?"

"With you?" Covering his hand with hers, she leaned her cheek into his palm and smiled. "Very possibly. You have a way about you, Logan Strong. You could make a woman forget she's past her prime and has stretch marks to prove it."

"You're a beautiful woman, Janice. Very desirable."

Her eyes fluttered closed. "The combination of

moonlight and bagpipes must be going to your head just as they are to mine.''

''No.'' Leaning forward, the wooden drones of his bagpipes clicking together as he moved, he brushed his lips to her closed eyelids, risking temptation again like an arsonist sparking one match after another, knowing eventually the tinder will burst into flame. ''Don't ever think that.''

''Then you don't mind that I'm practically throwing myself at your feet?''

''I can handle it.'' Barely, and only at great cost to his self-control.

She seemed to find some inner strength, lifted her chin at a determined angle and backed away. ''I suppose this means I may never find out what men really wear under those kilts.''

His lips twitched. ''Watch it, sweetheart. Once I reveal that, there's no turning back.''

''Then I'll make sure I know where I'm going before I begin exploring that topic on my own.''

A primal tremor of anticipation shuddered through Logan. The temptation to take Janice now, despite his qualms, was almost overwhelming. In recent weeks he'd spent too many hours thinking of her, too many nights dreaming of her in his arms. Even in the face of her apparent willingness, she wasn't available to him. Not really. And if she knew the truth—about his failure to stop Ray when he'd had the chance—she wouldn't want him at all.

''It's late,'' he said softly. ''Maybe we ought to call it a night.''

Janice almost flinched at his dismissal, however gentle his tone. What must Logan think of her? A desperate woman so anxious for a man's attention she'd practically begged him to make love to her. Only a modicum of pride had stopped her from doing just that.

Debbie had been right. She'd come close to making a fool of herself when all Logan had ever intended was friendship for the widow of a fellow firefighter.

But oh, that kiss had felt like so much more!

To her horror, tears sprang to her eyes. He'd given her a charity kiss, born of pity, not based on the sexual sizzle that had been hers alone. She'd misunderstood his generosity for something quite different, something that was a figment of her vivid imagination.

The lights on the north side of the lake blurred through her tears, dancing like fireflies on a hot summer evening in the midwest. That was something California lacked. Fireflies.

Apparently she lacked something more basic. Sex appeal. In recent years, Ray had certainly made it clear she didn't measure up in the bedroom.

Swallowing a sense of failure, she cleared her throat. "I imagine the kids will be up early and raring to go again."

"I'll have breakfast ready. Trout, hash browns and fruit."

"The children usually just have cereal and—"

"I've got some of that in reserve if the fish doesn't go over so well."

"You've already been so kind. I feel like I should be making breakfast for you."

"Maybe another time."

Janice would like to think she'd have that chance, an intimate morning, coffee and croissants in bed. But it wasn't very likely. Not in the foreseeable future.

Suddenly chilled, she shivered and finger-combed her hair back from her face. "You sure you'll be all right sleeping on the couch?"

"I'll be fine."

"Then, uh, goodnight. I'll see you in the morning."

He didn't speak as she walked away, and she didn't look back, but she knew he was standing alone on the dock, the perfect image of a heroic Scottish Highlander with his pipes.

THE COUCH was a full six inches too short. It wouldn't have mattered if it had been two feet longer. Logan had known he wouldn't get any sleep with Janice in the adjacent room. And he'd been right. He'd heard every move she'd made in his bed, heard every squeak of the springs. His unruly libido had sounded the call to action all night.

Ignoring the demands of his body had been pure torture.

When the first rays of morning sunlight gleamed off the lake, he gave up all pretense of trying to sleep. His muscles ached and his eyes were gluey with fatigue as he stood and stretched.

"I'm certainly glad you don't sleep in the altogether."

He whirled to find Janice standing at the hallway to the bedrooms, looking bright and chipper in shorts and a copper-colored blouse. The natural curls of her sable hair were combed into order, her makeup fresh. She created a vision he wished he'd wake up to every morning, and one that would be there every night as well.

How had he not heard her? Not sensed her presence or caught the sweet scent of her perfume?

Grateful he'd had the foresight to wear shorts to sleep in instead of being caught in the buff, he grabbed for the T-shirt he'd draped over the back of the couch. He pulled it on over his head. "I didn't hear you get up."

"It's such a beautiful day, it seemed like a waste to sleep late."

"Morning's my favorite time of day." He felt rooted to the spot, unable to move. Unable to take his eyes off her or to stop wishing he'd had a chance to kiss her awake.

Crossing the room, she paused in front of the window. "The lake's so still, it looks like glass."

Finally able to move, to breathe evenly, he said, "I'll fix us some coffee. We can take it out on the deck."

She glanced back over her shoulder. "After the way I acted last night, you must think I'm the most promiscuous woman in the county. I apologize."

"You? Promiscuous? That's not what I think."

"I practically begged you to make love to me right out there on the dock."

He cocked a brow. "Funny, I thought I was the one trying to seduce *you.*"

"But you had the good sense to stop before things got out of hand. I promise I won't force myself on you again." Her shoulders were very straight, her expression grim.

He marveled that she had taken the blame for their kiss, for him wanting her so badly he still ached with his need for her.

"Tell you what." He walked into the kitchen, plucked up a coffee filter and began to fill the pot with a special vanilla-flavored blend he liked. "Let's both make a promise not to apologize again for what happened last night."

"You're not upset with me? For being too forward?"

"Not a chance, sweetheart." He only regretted he didn't dare act on the urges they both were experiencing.

The tension eased from her shoulders. "Thank goodness for that. When I had a chance to think about it, I was so embarrassed."

"Don't be." He got down a couple of mugs from the cupboard. "Now then, why don't you grab those folding chairs in the corner, take them outside and find a nice place to sit while the coffee brews. I'll join you in a minute." Just as soon as his body simmered down from all the conversation about seduction.

"Good idea. The children will wake up soon. We might as well enjoy the quiet while we can."

A few minutes later, he carried the mugs out onto

the deck where she'd picked a shady spot for the chairs.

Their eyes met as he handed her the coffee, and he felt another punch in the gut when the smile of welcome sparked in her ginger-brown eyes.

"I love a man who's domestic," she teased.

"Self-preservation. My mother's a wonderful person but she can turn a hamburger patty into a hockey puck without even trying. I came to the realization early that if I wanted to eat a decent meal I'd have to learn to cook. Turned out I like doing it, and not just hamburgers and tacos, but the real gourmet stuff, too, like French cuisine." He settled into the chair beside Janice and stretched out his legs, crossing his bare feet at the ankles.

They sipped their coffee in comfortable silence. Across the lake, smoke drifted up from a couple of campfires, spreading lightly along the tops of the pine trees. Nearer at hand, a squirrel chattered his good morning and was answered by an ill-tempered Stellar's jay.

Logan smiled to himself. This is how mornings should always be—nature awakening from its slumber and a good woman beside him.

"Did you used to go camping when you were young?" Janice asked.

"Some. My dad was a pretty good fisherman, though Mom wasn't all that thrilled about cooking his catch." Idly, he ran his palm across his whiskers, his thoughts on earlier times. "My brother and I still go backpacking in the Sierras a couple of times a year.

Sometimes I think his wife is glad to get rid of him for a day or two.''

Janice chuckled. ''I admit there were days when I was relieved Ray was working a twenty-four-hour shift. Sometimes a woman needs to be alone.''

She turned, her gaze snaring his with sweet heat, and she gave him a wry smile. ''This isn't one of those times, if you were wondering.''

''I wasn't—''

A subtle vibration of the deck halted his thought.

''Logan!'' Maddie cried, racing toward him, barefooted and still in her nightgown with little pink bows. ''Do we gets to go fishing some more?''

He lifted his mug out of the way before she could topple the contents, and she took possession of his lap as if she owned it. Truth was, she owned that and a piece of his heart, too.

''I don't know, sprite. We'll have to ask your mom.''

Kevin, already dressed, arrived at a more sedate pace. ''Can I take the boat out by myself first? Just me without dork, here.''

''Kevin,'' his mother admonished. ''I don't like you calling your sister names. Besides, maybe Logan doesn't want you to take his boat.''

''It's all right with me. He can row around till I get breakfast ready.''

''Cool! Can I Mom?''

''I don't know.'' Janice hesitated. ''You'd have to promise to stay close to the dock and wear your life jacket.''

"Aw, Mom, I can swim—"

"Those are good rules, Kevin," Logan said. "*If* your mother says it's okay to go on your own." In Logan's view, Kevin could manage the rowboat, and a boy needed a chance to test his abilities.

With obvious reluctance, Janice nodded her approval. "But you be careful, you hear?"

In a flash, Kevin was on his way down the dock.

"I wanna go, too," Maddie pleaded. "I'll wear my life jacket, I promise."

Standing with Maddie still in his arms, Logan said, "Let's let Kevin try it alone first. I'll get him going, then you can help me cook breakfast. How's that?"

Maddie's scowl was a tiny replica of the one that sometimes crossed Janice's face when she was deep in thought. Logan almost laughed aloud.

Under Janice's cautious eye and Maddie's careful supervision, Logan got Kevin all set and gave the boat a gentle shove away from the dock. The boy lowered his oars into the water and looked up at Logan.

"I wish my dad were here to see me," he said.

The boy's solemn pronouncement, the longing in the child's eyes, slammed into Logan's gut. "Yeah. He'd be real proud of you."

As Kevin rowed a zigzag path through the water, Logan reminded himself that what happened, or didn't happen, between him and Janice affected more than just the two of them. There were kids involved, kids who had loved their father.

How would they react if they learned Logan carried some part of the burden of responsibility for their father's death?

Chapter Nine

Janice drove through the central part of the college campus and parked in a visitor's slot next to the building where KUCP, the school's public radio station, was housed. She'd been stunned to receive Kimberly Lydell's call a few days after her stay at Logan's house. Now she was a nervous wreck.

She'd only had one job interview since landing her part-time sandwich-making job in college, and that one hadn't gone particularly well.

Ray hadn't wanted her to work. With him gone and the enormous debts he'd left, now she had no choice but to work, and she was ill-equipped for the job market. The irony didn't escape her.

The yellow brick building had a classical look, solidly built with marble columns marking the main entrance and double-wide mahogany doors flanked by marble panels. Clashing with the nineteenth-century feel of the place, the radio tower gracelessly topped the three-story structure like a birthday candle stuck as an afterthought into a pan of lemon squares.

Two students burst out of the building as Janice

reached to open the door. Ponytail flying, her legs long and tan in a pair of tennis shorts, the girl giggled a quick, "Oops, sorry, ma'am."

The boy, who didn't look all that much older than Kevin, held the door open for Janice, making her feel ancient. Weakly, she smiled her thanks. At least his mother had taught him manners, and he'd remembered them when faced with what he apparently perceived as a doddering old woman. *Ma'am*, for heaven's sake! She was only thirty, though admittedly she'd aged a lot in the past month or so.

She sighed and went upstairs. Another student waved her into Kim's office—or rather into an over-size closet that contained a desk, two chairs and stacks of magazines and books covering every horizontal surface.

"Janice! I'm so glad to see you." Standing, Kim eased out from behind her desk. She gave Janice a warm hug, then without entirely releasing her, asked, "How are you doing?"

"I'm fine. Thanks to everyone sprucing up the place, I've sold the house."

"Jay told me. That was fast. The market must be something else again."

"Which creates this whole other problem of where we're going to live. The new buyers want us out of there in a hurry. We'll probably have to put our things in storage for a while, then camp out as best we can in an apartment."

"Oh, dear, that doesn't sound like much fun."

Janice shrugged. She'd dressed in the most professional outfit she owned, a pale green sheath dress with a short jacket, and heels. She hadn't expected to be swept up in a personal conversation, but she should have known. Kim was a truly genuine person, which was what made her late-night talk show so popular. She cared about every topic, every person who called.

She'd been just as popular as a local TV news anchor until she'd been injured, her face scarred during an earthquake. Nowadays, most people didn't even notice. Certainly Janice rarely did.

Kim gave her another squeeze. "While you're in between places to live, why don't you and the children stay with us? Jay and I have plenty of room."

Janice knew Kim and Jay lived in a beautiful house in the hills above Paseo, a far more elegant home than most firefighters could afford. Given how much they had both suffered with physical injuries—Kim's facial scarring and an accident that temporarily blinded Jay—Janice didn't resent their happiness now one iota.

"I wouldn't want to impose," she said. "The kids and I already moved in on Logan while the house was tented for termites."

Kim's honey-blond brows shot up. "You did?"

"It was only for one night." Wishing she had bitten her tongue instead of revealing that tidbit of news, Janice said, "He's been very kind to us since Ray died. Part of the brotherhood of firefighters, I'm sure."

"Hmm." Turning, Kim edged her way back behind her desk and gestured for Janice to sit in the straight-backed chair opposite her. "Jay's been worried about Logan. He's seemed so, I don't know, I guess *distant* would be the right word, since Ray's accident. Jay thinks Logan may feel guilty about what happened.''

''I hope that's not the case.'' Though Janice had wondered if his kindness—including the deep, lingering kiss she hadn't been able to put out of her mind—could have been a manifestation of his guilt. She'd hate that and hadn't been able to get the possibility out of her head.

''Whatever. There's no accounting for men and their reactions.'' Kim waved her hand in the air as if to dismiss the topic entirely. ''What I'm hoping is that you haven't found a job yet.''

''I had an interview at a temporary agency yesterday. The gentleman interviewing me suggested the results of my typing test weren't exactly encouraging,'' she admitted.

''Isn't that always the way? Some man takes one look at a woman and decides if she can't type she isn't worth squat.'' Kim shook her head. ''What I have in mind, if you're interested, is hiring you as a research assistant.''

Janice struggled valiantly not to let her jaw drop. ''Research assistant?''

''You said you were a history major and loved plowing through old books, that sort of thing. That's exactly what I need for my show, someone to dig up details and leads for me. Not history, really, but contemporary background material, coming up with ideas for interviews through newspapers, periodicals.'' Vaguely, she gestured around her cluttered office. ''What do you think?''

Thrilled with the idea, Janice was torn between a stomach that threatened to rebel at the excitement and relief of finding the perfect job, or jumping up to do a Scottish jig. "I think that would be wonderful. I'd love it."

"The station can't pay a whole lot." Naming a salary that wouldn't force Janice into a particularly high tax bracket, Kim looked apologetic. "You might be able to do better."

"Not likely." The salary was higher than she'd hoped for, and far more than she'd earn for flipping burgers, which was the fate she had feared.

"If you've got access to a computer, you can even do some of the research online at home, which ought to make it easier since you have your children to worry about."

Janice grinned. "You don't have to sell me on the job. When do I start?"

With a laugh, Kim said, "Whenever you'd like, though you might want to wait until your housing situation is settled. Moving can be stressful."

Delaying wasn't going to help her financial situation. Just yesterday she'd had another threatening letter from the Las Vegas casino where Ray had run up such a huge debt. Despite her trepidations, she knew she was going to have to face that problem head-on— and soon.

"Could you give me a week?" she asked.

"Perfect," Kim agreed. "Meanwhile I'll find you a desk and someplace to hang your hat—metaphorically speaking."

Janice's footsteps were a little lighter as she left the sturdy university building. She wasn't out of the financial woods yet. But knowing she'd be earning a decent salary would help her make a decision on her housing options. There was a small townhouse on the east side of town that would be available soon. It had three minuscule bedrooms and a postage-stamp yard where Janice could indulge her love of gardening on at least a small scale.

She sighed as she got into her sweltering-hot van. Once she had arranged a roof over her family's head, she'd have to deal with Las Vegas. That was a problem that wasn't going to go away.

LOGAN WANTED to celebrate.

He'd aced the written exam for engineer, the top scorer in the department.

His first call went to his dad. "Hey, Dad, how're you doing?"

"You know, some days are better than others. But I'm okay."

Logan pictured his father as he used to be—big and strong, with wide shoulders and a weight-lifter's physique, a man who could haul hose up a hundred-foot tower and not get winded. A father who could lift his son onto his shoulders. Now, cancer and chemotherapy had taken their toll, leaving a frail old man in his father's place.

"You'll lick this, Dad. Just hang in there."

"Doing the best I can. What's up with you?"

"They posted the results of the test."

"Yeah?" There was excitement in his father's voice.

"It was a pretty rough test," Logan hedged, dragging out the moment of triumph.

"So you got the top score, huh? Had to show up your brother, I suppose."

Logan grinned. "You got that straight."

"I'm proud of you, son."

As much as anything in his life, Logan wanted his dad to be the one to present him with an engineer's shield. He wanted his father to live that long—and longer.

They talked about his brother's kids and his mom's vegetable garden. Logan promised to come by the house in Paseo del Real on his next day off to help harvest the tomatoes that were overrunning the backyard. When his dad's voice began to sound weary, Logan told him good-bye and hung up.

He stood for a moment remembering all the good times and hoping for more, then pulled himself together.

Now he wanted to share the news with Janice. That wasn't a particularly smart plan, but he couldn't help himself. When good things happen, they need to be shared with special people

His dad was special. So was Janice.

At some deep level he'd never allowed to surface, he'd known that for years. When she'd showed up at an Open House at the fire station, or come to a department picnic at the park, he'd been aware of her. The way she moved, her quick smile. Her kids.

And how Ray had kept her at arm's length.

He'd tried not to think about that. He never would have made a move on another man's wife, especially not a firefighter's. That was strictly off limits.

Now Ray was gone, and Logan was so torn between wanting Janice for himself and feeling guilty that he was at fault for Ray's death, he could barely function.

He only knew he wanted Janice to help him celebrate getting one rung closer to following in his father's footsteps.

Parking in front of her house, he wasn't even sure he'd find her at home until he spotted her van parked in the driveway. The kids would be at school, Maddie for another hour, Kevin till three when soccer practice started. But Logan wanted to see Janice now. He'd stayed away for four days. That's all a man could handle.

He took the porch steps in one leap, punched the doorbell and tried to ignore the knot in his stomach.

She opened the door, appearing like a beautiful surreal painting behind the screen, all muted greens and soft browns. "Logan, what are you doing—"

"I took a chance you'd be—"

"I just got back—"

"There was something I wanted to tell you."

"I have news, too."

Unlatching the screen, she pushed it open and he stepped inside. It was all he could do not to pick her up, twirl her around. Kiss her.

"You look great," he said.

She flushed. "I had a job interview this morning."

"Yeah? I bet you wowed 'em."

"I don't know about that. It was with Kim Lydell— Jay's wife." Janice's smile broadened and her eyes sparked with both pride and pleasure. "She hired me to work for KUCP radio. I'm no longer among the ranks of the unemployed."

"Hey, that's great! Does that mean I get to listen to your sexy voice on the radio?"

Laughing, Janice felt the heat of a blush race up her neck to flush her cheeks. "Don't be silly. I don't have a sexy—"

"Yes, you do. At least, I think so. Kind of soft and sultry. Very sexy."

Her heart did an excited tap dance against her rib cage. No one had ever told her she had a sexy anything, and now Logan, who was only a "friend," thought her voice, of all things, was sexy. It left her momentarily speechless.

"So, if you're not going to be on-air talent, what are you going to do?" he persisted.

"Um, research. For Kim. Line up people to interview. That sort of thing."

"You'll be terrific. Congratulations."

"Thanks." Regaining her mental equilibrium, if not entirely her objectivity, she hooked her arm through his. "You can help me celebrate. Coffee? Iced tea? Or something stronger?"

"Iced tea sounds perfect."

Together they walked into the kitchen, Janice vitally aware of the flex of Logan's strong arm beneath her hand, his far greater height than hers even though she was wearing heels, and the spicy fragrance of his aftershave mingled with a masculine scent that was specifically his own. A combination, she thought, of sunshine, pine forests and pure sex appeal. A dizzying gourmet blend designed to entice a woman to forget herself.

"You said you have some news, too?" she asked, reluctant to disengage from the warmth that emanated from him. She was in no hurry to produce a pitcher of iced tea at the cost of losing her tenuous physical contact with Logan. For the past four days, she'd desperately missed seeing him. Foolishly so.

He grinned. "I nailed the written exam for engineer. Top score in the city."

"Oh, Logan, that's wonderful! We both have something to celebrate." Without thinking, she raised up to give him a quick kiss.

As though he'd been waiting for just that, he took control, capturing her lips with his. She gasped in surprise and pleasure as his heat seared her. Elation coiled in her midsection. And then the kiss was over, leaving her breathless, her senses reeling.

Dear heaven! If that was a kiss of friendship, she'd never survive one he meant as a lover. But given a chance, she'd die a happy woman.

"So," he said, apparently far more under control than she, "when do you start work?"

"Um, a week. I asked her for a week." Never had she felt more bewildered by a man or by her own reactions. "I also put a deposit down on a townhouse this morning. The timing isn't a perfect match but we'll manage. And I figured I'd need the week to get things moved into storage temporarily and to take a trip to Las Vegas.''

His sandy-brown eyebrows shot up. "Vegas?"

Now, with the reminder of Ray's debts resting squarely on her shoulders, she was able to turn away from Logan. Move away to the cupboard where she kept the tea.

"I feel like I'll do better if I see the casino manager in person. Basically, my debts are still bigger than what few assets I've got." She reached for the pitcher and fussed, mixing instant tea and water. Probably not as gourmet as Logan was used to, but instant was all she had. "I thought if I could talk to him eye-to-eye, not just some voice on the other end of the phone line, I could convince him that one of two things would happen. I could declare bankruptcy, which would mean he wouldn't get any of Ray's gambling debts back. Or he could agree that I'll pay the money back on some sort of an installment plan that I can afford. That way I'll be able to handle the full down payment on the townhouse. Otherwise, we'll be in a rental unit somewhere living month to month.''

"You shouldn't have to pay Ray's debts back at all.''

At Logan's angry tone, she glanced back over her shoulder. "He was my husband. This is a community property state, including the debts. I think I'm stuck." And she wouldn't want to burden any other man with that responsibility. Although she wouldn't mind if Ms. Purple Thongs got stuck with the bill. Evidently she'd had the fun of running up the tab. "Of course, it would be nice if I could convince the casino to forget the whole thing." Everyone needed a pipe dream, she thought wryly.

"Maybe you should consult an attorney."

"I hate to spend more money on top of what I already owe. If I can settle things on my own, I'll be better off. And I intend to be a tough negotiator."

As though he felt at home in her kitchen, he found the glasses and plopped ice into them, setting them on the counter beside the pitcher of tea she'd made.

"I'll go with you to Vegas."

"You don't have to—"

"I'm going, Janice. Don't even try to talk me out of it."

"You can't just willy-nilly take off. You have your work. And don't you have an oral exam coming up for the promotion? You can't miss—"

"That's not till next week, and I can rearrange my work schedule easily enough. When do you want to leave?"

Janice hadn't realized what a stubborn man Logan could be. That he'd be so determined to help her warmed a spot deep inside her that was perilously close to her heart.

TWO DAYS LATER, with the eastern sky just beginning to lighten with the coming of dawn, Logan placed Janice's overnight case next to his duffel bag in the trunk of his Mustang. The children were staying at a neighbor's. If all went well, Logan expected to have Janice back home by the time Kevin was out of school the following afternoon.

For the one night they'd be together, he'd made reservations for adjoining rooms at the Vegas hotel where Ray had gambled away Janice's security.

He wished instead they'd be sharing a single room with a king-size bed.

His jaw clenched. *Not gonna happen,* he reminded himself.

In the passenger seat, Janice snapped her seatbelt in place. ''This is the first time I've gone away and left the children.''

He twisted the key in the ignition, gratified by the low rumble of the engine's response, and glanced at Janice. ''Then it's high time you had a vacation.''

''I'll probably worry about them the whole time I'm gone even though I know Debbie is perfectly capable of taking good care of them. Silly, isn't it?''

''Nope. Sounds exactly like a typical mother who loves her kids.''

Her lips curved into one of her gentle smiles. ''Thanks for coming with me. I'm glad I don't have to do this alone.''

Reaching over, he rested a reassuring hand on her thigh. Her skin warmed his palm through the cotton fabric of her skirt, the spaghetti tank top she wore bared shoulders smoothly tanned by the summer's sun. Her dark hair, freshly washed, gleamed in the reflected light of the rising sun.

The car had already filled with her subtle floral fragrance, a light perfume that made him think of the garden she'd tended so lovingly, a garden that would soon belong to another woman. Another family.

If he could, he'd bring Ray back to life—and drive his fist right through the guy's jaw for having put Janice through so much pain. As it was, Logan would have to concentrate extra hard on his driving to avoid being distracted by the lovely woman sitting next to him.

Keenly alert to both what was happening inside and outside the car, Logan let the big engine under the hood eat up the highway miles.

Sitting back, Janice tried to relax and enjoy the ride. It wasn't easy. Anxiety gnawed at her stomach, making her wish she hadn't bothered with breakfast. What would happen if the casino manager refused to negotiate? If they took her to court? That would drain everything she had and eat into whatever income she could generate.

Unwilling to spend the entire trip to Vegas fretting over her precarious future, she shifted in her seat and said, "I assume you've been to Las Vegas before?"

"Once. There was a pipe and drum corps competition there a few years back."

"Did your band win?"

He grimaced. "Second place. A group from Seattle beat us out. Bad judging."

She laughed. "We're not just a little competitive, are we, and maybe a tiny bit prejudiced?"

"Certainly not," he scoffed. "Everyone I know thought we performed better than they did. We should have won."

"I'm sure you should have, too." Logan never did anything half-way, she realized. He'd take playing his pipes just as seriously as he took his work as a fire-fighter putting out a fire. In both cases he'd make sure he won, beat down the enemy. It was simply who he was, and she loved him for it.

Startled by the thought, she drew in a sharp breath. Had she truly gone that far? Two months widowed and she'd already lost her heart to another man?

Why not? she wondered. Hadn't Ray walked away from her both physically and emotionally long before his death? Hardly a surprise that she'd attach herself to the first man who paid her any attention.

But Logan was far more than that. He was kind and caring with her, wonderful with her children. And his kisses—

Despite the apologies on both sides, those kisses *had* to mean something. Hers certainly did. All the more now that she realized how far into love with Logan she'd allowed herself to slide.

Which meant she had to be all the more careful not to step over the line, both for his sake and hers. She couldn't—wouldn't—burden Logan with her financial troubles. Nor did she want to risk a broken heart.

A lump caught in her throat, and she realized she might already be too late to prevent her own heartache.

Struggling to focus on something else, she asked, "So did you try your hand at gambling in Vegas while you were there?"

"I dropped a few quarters into the slots, and saw a

show or two. I'm not much for throwing my money away.''

She nodded. ''Too bad Ray didn't feel the same way.''

Slanting her a glance, he smiled. ''Try not to worry, Jan. I've got a good feeling about this trip. Things are going to work out. You'll see.'' His grin broadened. ''For what it's worth, Emma Jean predicted we'd both come home winners.''

Fighting an unwelcome press of tears, she hoped Logan was right. But she didn't dare give credence to Emma Jean's earlier prediction that she and Logan had matrimony in their futures. Surely that was too much to hope for.

SINCE HIS LAST TRIP to Las Vegas, the hotels along the strip had become bigger and taller and even more glittering. Despite the heat of midafternoon, pedestrians thronged up and down the street in search of excitement. A few managed to get their thrills by dashing through the heavy traffic, risking life and limb.

Logan shook his head as he finally managed to turn left across the traffic into the hotel parking lot, narrowly missing a taxi that had barreled straight in front of him. This was a crazy town. If it weren't for Janice, he'd be happy to do an about-face and head back to Lake Almador right now.

''What time is your appointment with the casino manager?'' he asked as he wedged the Mustang between a Mercedes 500S and a pickup truck.

''Three-thirty. I hoped that would give me time to

wash up and change into something that looks like I'm on the brink of poverty. Maybe it would go quicker if I just showed him my checkbook."

His lips twitched. "If I'd known your plan, I would have brought my old painting clothes. The ones with the holes in them."

"Oh, well, if this doesn't work we can always try panhandling on the strip. Where do people get so much money they can just throw it away on a roulette table?"

Logan didn't know the answer to that one. Maybe for some it was that same adrenaline high he got when the fire tone sounded. He knew the risks and was willing to take a chance with his life.

Ray had understood the risks, too. So why the hell had he blown his money gambling, and then virtually walked into a hell hole of fire despite Logan's warning shout that the roof was about to collapse?

Too bad he'd never get the answer to that question.

Getting their gear out of the trunk, Logan escorted Janice toward the hotel entrance. He'd noted a sign down the street announcing the temperature was a hundred-and-ten degrees. Even at ninety degrees, it was brush-fire weather in Paseo, a danger every year in early fall. Here, there wasn't much brush to burn.

Cool air and a room full of slot machines with ringing bells and cascading coins dropping into metal trays greeted them as they stepped through the entrance to the hotel and casino. They made their way through the maze of machines toward the registration desk, that area marginally quieter than the casino, the sounds muted by plush carpets, potted plants and marble columns, more slot machines discreetly placed around the perimeter.

"This is incredible," Janice whispered, as though in awe of the opulent display. She caught his arm. "I'm not sure I can afford to stay here for even one night. Maybe we should—"

"Honey, the rooms are cheaper here than they are at the seedy motels downtown. They make all the profits they need at the tables." He headed directly for the registration desk.

Janice, he noticed, lingered back from the counter, uncomfortable, he supposed, registering at a hotel with a man who wasn't her husband. She wasn't the kind who did that sort of thing. To Logan's chagrin, however much he appreciated her high standards and morals, this was one time he wished Janice was a little more liberated. One room—and one bed—would do them both just fine, if she were willing.

And he had no right to be thinking that.

Paperwork completed, he declined the help of a bellboy and turned to see Janice standing right where she'd stopped at the edge of the carpet. Except now her face was as pale as a ghost, her eyes wide and staring straight ahead.

He glanced around the lobby but didn't detect anything out of the ordinary except a guy in drag followed by an entourage of groupies. A dinner club performer, he surmised, and not all that unusual in Vegas.

"What's wrong?" he asked when he reached Janice.

She swallowed visibly. "I want to go to my room. Please. Now."

"Sure." He juggled their bags so he had a free hand, and he looped his arm around her waist. "Are you okay?"

She simply shook her head and headed off in the wrong direction. He wheeled her around to the elevators. They rode up with three other people, nobody making eye contact, nobody talking. He got out on the seventh floor, knowing a fire ladder would reach that high, and ushered her toward their rooms.

She still hadn't spoken when he'd opened the door and let her inside. Instead, she walked directly across the room to stare out the window.

"Okay, you're scaring me. What's going on?"

It took a long time, but she finally turned around, a desperate look in her eyes, a wild look.

"She's downstairs. I saw her."

Maybe the long drive had slowed his mental processes but he didn't get it. "Who's downstairs?"

"The blonde I saw at Ray's funeral. The one who wears purple thong panties and Mango Madness lipstick."

Chapter Ten

Janice couldn't catch her breath. Her heart felt as if it were going to explode. Alternately, she went hot and cold, sweat beading on her forehead, between her breasts, then a blast of the air-conditioning chilled her, sending gooseflesh racing down her back and across her bare arms.

"Are you talking about the woman Ray was seeing?" Logan's eyes narrowed and his brows lowered into a concerned line.

She swallowed the bile that rose in her throat and nodded.

"She's downstairs?"

"At the car rental counter. She w-works here."

His big hands closed around her shoulders, holding her gently. "You can't know it's her. Vegas is full of blondes."

"I know." Dear God, at the funeral Janice had thought the woman was a co-worker, a city employee. A friend of Ray's. Only when those awful panties appeared, the telling lipstick, had she realized the total depth of Ray's betrayal. "She was his mistress."

He pulled her into his arms. But she was rigid, as fragile as an icicle and just as cold. Even his heat couldn't warm her.

"What do you want to do?"

"I don't know." She wanted to tear the woman's eyes out, to brand her with a big scarlet A. But mostly Janice wanted to know why she hadn't been enough for her husband. Why she had failed as a woman.

"I think you ought to leave it alone, sweetheart. It's the past. You need to get on with your future."

She barked a pitiful imitation of a laugh. "Some future. Ray and that—that woman left my future on the blackjack table, or wherever they played their games. How could he have done that to me? To his own children?"

"Gambling's an addiction for some people. Maybe he couldn't help himself."

"That's no excuse for taking up with th-that blonde." She shoved away from Logan and wiped her eyes, which were dry and grainy with fatigue. "I've got to see Mr. Bonelli, the casino manager. And then—" She shook her head.

"And then?"

"I can only deal with one problem at a time. Right now I need to wash my face and change clothes. So please—" With her fingertips, she touched his cheek, hoping to reassure both of them. "Please go. I'll be all right. Really I will."

He caught her hand, kissed the backs of her fingers. "I'll unlock my side of the adjoining door. If you need me—"

"I'll know how to find you. Thank you," she whispered. "Thank you for being here."

He picked up his duffel from the double bed where he'd dropped it, studied her a moment as if reluctant to leave, then walked to the door. With his hand on the knob, he said, "I'll change, too, and be ready when you are."

"Give me a half hour."

He nodded and left. A moment later she heard the door rattle in the adjacent room. Only then did she allow a sob to rise in her throat.

Ray's death and the subsequent funeral had been painful days filled with conflicting emotions; she suspected today would be even more difficult. Thank goodness Logan would be there to hold her if she came apart.

ARNOLD BONELLI'S office was as posh as the lobby had been, a thick carpet, an oversize desk and a wall filled with TV monitors that silently displayed various sections of the casino. The manager, who had dark, slicked-back hair and a generous girth, appeared typecast as a Mafia don. But his smile seemed warm enough as he ushered them into his office, his demeanor unthreatening.

Janice could only hope Mr. Bonelli didn't believe in breaking people's knees if they couldn't pay off their debts.

She shook his hand and introduced Logan, exaggerating slightly by referring to him as a representative of the Paseo del Real Fire Department.

"I was sorry to hear of your loss, Mrs. Gainer," he said when the formalities were finished. He gestured to the leather chairs in front of his desk. "Mr. Gainer was one of our regular patrons."

She took the seat offered her, and found herself nearly swallowed by the upholstery. She scooted to the edge of the chair. "A little too regular, I gather."

Logan sat next to her. Noting her posture, the straight line of her spine, the determined tilt of her chin, he considered warning the casino manager that he was about to meet his match. No way was Janice going to fork over a dime of the money her husband had lost at the casino's tables without a battle. She would protect her interests and those of her children, even at the cost of spilling her own blood, he suspected.

But instead of warning Bonelli, Logan relaxed, ready to watch the show. Amazing how the modest dress she wore with a matching jacket in a pale green made her appear invincible—a Joan of Arc in cotton and silk.

Bonelli took his seat behind his desk. "I had an occasion or two to speak with your husband before his untimely death. I usually make an effort to meet our high rollers."

"What I don't understand," Janice said, "nor would the mayor and other officials in Paseo del Real—is how you allowed a firefighter to run up the kind of debt Ray managed. I would have thought you'd put limits on your, ah, patrons who obviously couldn't afford to lose that much."

The manager tented his fingers beneath his chin. "I was unaware of your husband's occupation until recently, Mrs. Gainer. And until the last few months of his life, Mr. Gainer had always paid his debts in a timely fashion. I had no reason to question his request to extend him additional credit."

"Until now," Janice said. "I don't have enough money to pay his debts, Mr. Bonelli, and it's unlikely I'll have enough in the foreseeable future. As I see it, I'll either have to declare bankruptcy or make some financial arrangements with you to reduce my obligation."

Logan smiled at the way she'd laid her cards on the table. She was betting she had a winning hand.

"Arrangements?" Bonelli questioned.

"Are you aware my husband died a hero's death?" she asked.

The manager's gaze slid to Logan, almost as if he was measuring the hint of a threat in Janice's voice, then he returned his attention to Janice. "I am now. Following your phone call, I did some checking."

"It seems to me it would be a PR disaster if the casino forced the widow of a brave firefighter who died in the line of duty into bankruptcy," she continued. "The news would certainly leak out. Your patrons might question how they would be treated if—"

Bonelli held up his hand. "I understand what you're saying."

"While the amount of money involved is substantial for me and my *children*—" she emphasized the word none too subtly "—compared to the daily receipts of a place like this—'' Shrugging, she let the thought hang in the air like a sharply honed sword. ''I'm sure you'll agree, my family and I would create a sympathetic picture if the newspapers got hold of the story. Casino Sends Widow into Bankruptcy would make an unattractive headline.''

Logan swallowed another smile, this one filled with admiration. Janice was one tough negotiator, and he reminded himself not to go head-to-head with her in any contract dealings. He'd far rather have her on his side.

Arrangement, phooey! She was aiming to get herself entirely off the hook.

Bonelli leaned back in his chair. ''I assure you, we have no desire to add to your difficulties, Mrs. Gainer. Although we don't have a set policy in matters of this sort, we are allowed a certain amount of flexibility— in the interests of good public relations, you understand.''

Logan nodded. Bonelli recognized Janice had dealt herself a royal flush. He was ready to fold.

Janice's heart leapt up into her throat. He was going to settle!

''While the amount is substantial by any definition, an organization of our size is better able to handle such a loss—''

''And is insured for that loss?'' Logan asked.

The tiniest hint of a smile played at the corners of the manager's lips. ''Sound business practice requires every organization carry certain types of insurance to protect against unforeseen loss.''

A buzz started in Janice's head. She wanted to jump up and click her heels together but restrained herself. Instead she simply enjoyed the giddy sense of relief as it fizzed through her veins like potent champagne.

By the time she shook hands with Mr. Bonelli and said goodbye, she realized she'd come out of her financial crisis with money in the bank, a solid nest egg to provide herself with security and her children with a chance for an education. The remaining credit-card debts Ray had incurred were still huge but at least manageable.

Thank God!

Back in the lobby, Logan grinned at her. ''The guy even comped our rooms. Not bad for an afternoon's work. You were terrific.''

''Not bad at all.'' She squeezed his hand. ''Thanks.''

''Hey, I didn't do anything.''

''You were there for me. I figured if he decided to break somebody's knees, he'd have to go through you to get to me.''

His eyebrows shot up in surprise.

As she laughed, her gaze slid toward the car rental counter, and the blonde sitting behind it. Her throat tightened.

''Logan, there's something else I have to do. Why don't you go to the bar, order us some drinks, and I'll be there in a minute?''

He followed her gaze. ''Just leave it, Jan. Nothing's going to change.''

"I know. This is something I have to do alone. It won't take me long."

"I'll go with you."

"No, this is between me and that woman. Just the two of us." When she saw the concern in his gentle hazel eyes, she smiled. "I promise I won't make a scene. I might pull out a few clumps of hair," she conceded, "but I won't spill a single drop of blood."

"Okay, but if anything goes wrong, I'll be there to bail you out of the slammer."

Taking a deep breath, she turned and walked across the wide lobby, past ornate marble columns and potted plants, noisy slot machines clicking and clacking, people laughing.

It was one of the longest walks she'd taken in her life. This was going to be much more difficult than dealing with something as impersonal as a gambling debt. This was the heart and soul of who she had been as a woman.

She stopped in front of the car rental counter. The woman's name tag read Christie Greene and her golden-blonde hair was pulled back into a sophisticated chignon.

Hate and jealousy mingled with the bile in Janice's throat and the desperate sense of betrayal.

The woman looked up, a practiced smile on her face but no recognition in her eyes. "May I help you?"

"I'm Janice Gainer, Ray's wife."

The woman's expression crumbled, and a blush bloomed on her cheeks. Her gaze darted around the lobby as though in search of help.

"I'm not going to create a scene. It's just that I—" Janice faltered. What did she want from this woman? An apology? Or to humble her as she'd humbled Janice? Not exactly a noble goal.

"I'm so sorry," Christie whispered, her voice velvet soft.

"Because you had an affair with my husband?"

"Yes. At first I didn't—" Her chin trembled. "Ray didn't wear a wedding ring."

He'd always told Janice a ring would be dangerous on the job. Now she suspected that was only an excuse so he could philander with other women. Oh, God, how that hurt!

"But when you found out he was married, you didn't do anything about it, did you?" she said, her accusation sharp and cutting.

"No, I didn't. I tried not to see him again, but I couldn't seem to stay away. By then, I—" She broke off and tears filled her eyes. "I know it's no excuse, but by then I loved him."

To Janice's dismay, she found herself sympathizing with Christie. That wasn't fair. She had every right to hate the woman. At some level, she did. Bitterly. But now, with Ray gone, it seemed like a wasted emotion.

"But I'm sorry for more than just our affair."

Slowly, Janice raised her brows. "What could be worse than carrying on with a married man?"

Behind the counter, Christie straightened some of the car rental brochures and set them aside as though trying to organize her thoughts. "Before he died, he'd lost a lot of money at the tables and he kept falling deeper and deeper in debt.''

"I'm aware of that—now.''

"He kept trying to find a way out, to get even, doubling his bets when he lost, which only made things worse.''

"He could have stopped altogether.''

"I know. I suggested that, but he wouldn't listen. He kept talking about the hole he'd dug for himself and how that was going to hurt you and your children.''

Janice's jaw went slack. "Ray talked about us?''

"Often—once he'd let it slip that he had a family. He was so worried.'' Rearranging another stack of brochures, Christie's hands began to tremble so badly she dropped them, scattering them behind the counter. She bent down to scoop them up, then appeared to give up the effort altogether. "One night I mentioned that the casino often wiped out the debts of someone who died, if it was a special case, if the family—'' She covered her mouth with her hand. "Oh, God, I never should have told him.''

An uneasiness crept along Janice's spine. "What are you saying?''

"A week after I told him that, he came back. He was wild that night, trying to recoup his losses. He tried roulette, which wasn't his usual game, and he only lost more. It was like he'd gone mad. He played every table, took huge risks. It didn't make any sense to me until—'' Pursing her lips together, she closed her eyes. A single tear edged down her cheek. "Until

I heard the next day that a firefighter in Paseo del Real had died on the job. Then I knew that Ray had—''

''Killed himself?'' Janice said with a gasp.

''I felt so guilty. If he hadn't thought the casino would forgive his gambling debts...'' She sobbed, tried to catch her breath. ''I'm so, so sorry—about everything.''

Janice didn't know how to react. She'd never considered that Ray might have wanted to die in that fire, or that he'd been concerned about her and the children at all.

Tears of confusion and grief brimmed in her eyes. Her throat felt tight, making it impossible for her to speak. Tentatively she covered Christie's hand and squeezed gently. She didn't want to absolve the woman of her guilt, but they'd both suffered a loss. Their mutual grief could be shared.

HE'D WAITED at the bar so long, Logan figured he'd have to order a second beer or go looking for Janice. He opted for the second choice.

Tossing a few bucks on the counter, he stood just as Janice came into the cocktail lounge. He couldn't read her expression, but she didn't look happy.

''We need to talk,'' she said without preamble.

''Talk?''

''You and me. I want to know what happened the day Ray died, and I want to know the truth.''

Logan took a step back as though he'd taken a punch to the solar plexus. He'd never wanted Janice to know the details of that morning. Couldn't imagine what the blonde had said to make Janice so insistent upon knowing the truth. But she was Ray's wife. He couldn't lie to her, not in the face of her determined questioning.

He glanced around. The lounge hadn't filled up yet. That would come later for the dinner show. Now there were only a few customers taking a break from the slots and assorted other games designed to separate them from their money.

He motioned toward an empty table in the shadows away from any other tables. What he had to say, he didn't want the world to hear. Then he gestured to the bartender to send a couple of beers to that table.

By the time they were seated, the waitress showed up with the beers. Janice silently acknowledged the drinks and took a sip from the glass the waitress had half filled from the bottle.

"Tell me," she said.

Logan took his time pouring the rest of his beer into his glass, watching the head form as he gathered his thoughts.

"Ray got to the station late that morning," he began. "That wasn't unusual for him, but it plays havoc with the guy on the prior shift. He can't leave till he passes off his assignment to the next guy, one-on-one, which means maybe he can't get home for breakfast in time to see his wife off to work. Or see his kids before they go to school."

"What about Ray?"

Mentally Logan tried to focus on that morning. Every detail he'd been trying so hard to forget.

"He hadn't been in the station five minutes when we got the run. That old warehouse down on Broadway. We'd been there before. Vagrants used it as a hangout. It should have been torn down years ago."

"It's still there, what's left of it," she commented.

"Yeah, and still a fire trap waiting to happen." Instead of the city tearing it down themselves, they'd been arguing with the owners about liability. Nobody wanted to foot the bill, but somebody would eventually. Logan could only hope it wouldn't be at the cost of another firefighter's life.

"We were first on the scene but the fire was going pretty good when we got there," he said, his memories returning to that morning. "While we were rolling, Ray acted like he was hungover. He said he'd been up all night." Logan glanced out toward the lobby where the blonde worked. "He'd driven back from Vegas."

Janice's eyes lowered to her beer, and she used her fingertip to draw a line down the frosted glass. "Yes. She told me. She said—" Her voice cracked, and she looked away. "Go on, please."

"He seemed punchy, sort of out of it. Not at top form, you know?"

She raised her head. "Depressed?"

Logan considered the question as he sipped his beer, trying to wash away the bitter memories that had been taunting him for the past two months.

"I thought—I thought he was still drunk. I should have—" His hand closed around his glass so tightly, he thought it might shatter. "When the battalion chief sent us up to vent the roof, I should have stopped Ray from even going up the ladder. He was in no condition to—''

''What happened on the roof?''

''I'm not sure. It seemed so routine until—'' The images rose in his memory. ''It was like he was moving in slow motion. Ray hesitated a second before he walked across the roof, his ax in hand, something determined about the way he held himself. He didn't look side to side, checking for hot spots, nothing like he should. I thought he just didn't give a damn. I thought he was still drunk out of his skull.''

Logan looked up when he felt Janice's hand cover his. Only then did he realize there were tears running down his cheeks. Janice, who had lost her husband, was comforting *him,* the man who hadn't done enough to save him.

''When I spotted the bubbling tar, I yelled at him. I swear I did. He didn't stop. He just kept on walking. He should have realized—'' Logan nearly strangled on a sob, the nightmare images so vivid in his mind. ''The roof gave out from under his feet.''

With incredible sadness, so softly Logan could barely hear her, Janice said, ''It wasn't your fault. I think he wanted to die.''

He sat in stunned silence unable to take in her meaning. ''Not that way. No one wants to die—''

''Christie thinks it's her fault.''

''Christie? Christie who? I don't get it.''

Sitting in stunned disbelief, Logan listened to what the blonde had told Janice. About Ray's mounting debts. His worry about Janice and the kids. And his escape route.

"That's why Christie came to the funeral," Janice concluded. "Out of love…and guilt."

Logan swore under his breath.

"We've all been accepting the guilt for Ray's death and we shouldn't have," Janice said. "He was responsible. And his addiction to gambling, if that's what it was."

And his addiction to another woman, Logan suspected, but he wouldn't voice that opinion. "I still should have stopped him."

"If you'd had a tank up there on the roof, I doubt you could have stopped him. He thought he'd found a way out, one that wouldn't hurt me or the children too much. He simply didn't understand…." Her voice hitched again.

Logan couldn't stand it. The bar was beginning to fill and this was no place for Janice, not when she was dealing with such powerful emotions.

"Come on, let's get out of here. I'll take you upstairs. You can rest—"

"No." She lifted her chin to what he recognized as a stubborn angle. "Ray's last thoughts were of his family. Whatever his faults—and they were obviously many—he didn't want me to spend the rest of my life in misery. I need to celebrate that, Logan. I need to validate that *life,* however difficult, is a better choice than death."

He wasn't quite sure he understood, but he had to give Janice credit. He couldn't imagine, even after fac-

ing a thousand fires, how much more courage it took
for her to face the reality of her husband's death and
make a conscious decision to move on. To make a life
for herself and her children.

"Would dinner with champagne do it?" he asked
softly.

"Perfect," she said, her chin trembling.

THE FIRST GLASS of champagne went right to her head.
The second one made her feel giddy. Having once
made the decision to look forward, not back, to rid
herself of guilt over Ray's death, the sense of relief
was like a rebirth.

Apparently rebirth as an adolescent because she felt
like she'd been sipping an aphrodisiac.

Although Logan had offered to take her to a dinner
show, even if he had to bribe someone for tickets, she
opted to eat in the restaurant where they could talk.
She didn't want the distraction of a stand-up comic or
a chorus of beautiful, half-naked women.

She simply wanted to cherish the exhilarating sense
of freedom—freedom from overwhelming debt and,
temporarily, freedom from the responsibilities of being
a mother.

But even more than that, she wanted to steal a few
hours alone with Logan, to be a woman with a man
she held as dear. A man she loved.

She forced herself to stifle a sigh. Logan was such
a perfect gentleman, her love was likely to go unre-
quited despite the romantic candlelight and mood music being played by a small combo. Only a few cou-

rageous couples had ventured onto the tiny dance floor.

Too bad she'd forgotten—or had never learned—how to be seductive.

Logan lifted the bottle of champagne from the bucket. "More?" A gentle smile played at the corners of his lips, and flame from the candle reflected in his eyes, turning them from hazel to a deeper brown.

She covered her glass with her hand. "I think I've probably had enough. I'd hate for you to have to carry me up to my room because I wasn't capable of walking."

His smile turned amused. "We firefighters are trained for that. Carrying you seven floors would be a snap."

"But don't you generally carry fire victims *down* the stairs rather than up?"

"In this case, though I'm sure I could manage, I'd consider using the elevator."

She laughed. He seemed more relaxed now than he had since Ray's death, as if revealing what had happened that dreadful morning had been as cathartic for him as it had been freeing for her.

All along she'd been afraid that he blamed himself, his concern for her a result of guilt.

Now she knew that was the case.

What she didn't know was if he had any other feelings for her.

The waiter arrived to remove their plates. She hadn't done her coq au vin justice; Logan had demolished every bit of his roast duck with orange sauce, the whole time wondering aloud if he could replicate the seasonings.

"May I bring you the dessert tray?" the waiter inquired with deference.

She met Logan's gaze. "Not for me. I couldn't eat another bite."

"Coffee?" he asked, and she nodded, wanting to linger with him.

When the waiter left, he said, "We could dance while we wait for the coffee."

Her eyes widened in surprise. "Oh, no, I couldn't. I haven't danced in years. I'd probably trample all over your toes."

"Neither have I." He stood, extending his hand. "Which means your toes will be at greater risk than mine. I'm willing to take the chance if you are."

Despite her hesitancy, Janice allowed herself to be drawn to her feet. She doubted Logan would be awkward at any activity, including dancing. She couldn't say the same for herself.

But before she knew it, she was in his arms, moving effortlessly as he led her around the small dance floor, her right hand tucked into his left, nearly invisible when his fingers closed around hers. At the small of her back, his broad palm heated through her dress to warm her flesh.

And her heart.

She breathed in his scent. The familiar fragrance of his spicy aftershave, the sun-fresh smell of detergent on the collar of his shirt. The elemental essence of a man. In the same primal way, she responded as a woman.

A tiny shudder rippled through her, and she rested her head on his shoulder, closing her eyes. But she wasn't relaxed. If anything she was hyper-alert as his hand slid lower on her back to her hips, pressing her closer, nestling her more firmly into the cradle of his hips where she felt—

Her feet tangled.

The telling bulge against her midsection jolted her. Her spirits soared, and for the first time in many years she felt the power of being a woman. She felt the owner of the moment, a co-conspirator with a long feminine line that led back to Eve. She rejoiced in the knowledge that Logan wanted her in the same way she wanted him, and she was humbled by the realization.

And afraid. Afraid he wouldn't want to take this feeling to the next step. That if he did, she wouldn't be able to please him.

The band segued into another slow number. It didn't matter. They didn't seem to be moving around the dance floor any longer but only swaying to a beat that thrummed low in her body, echoing his heavy heartbeat she felt where her palm rested against his chest. In counterpoint, a riot of sensations sped through her. The heat that surrounded her. The building tension. The ache of wanting that filled every cell, every atom of her existence.

The music stopped, the band leader announcing the combo was taking a break.

Logan didn't let her go but continued to hold her close, there on the empty dance floor. Vaguely, she wondered if anyone noticed. But she didn't really care. It simply felt too good to be this close to Logan.

"Maybe we should skip the coffee," he whispered in her ear.

Excitement crowded in her throat so painfully, she could barely respond. Barely breathe. Surely this was the invitation she'd been hoping for. "Yes."

"We have to get up early. It's a long ride back home tomorrow."

"Yes." But tonight was what she cared about. Tomorrow, somehow, would have to take care of itself.

Slowly, he released her, his hand sliding down her arm, his fingers linking with hers as they walked off the dance floor. In a few quick motions, he signed the check the waiter had left on the table and they made their way out of the restaurant.

Dozens of well-dressed hotel guests gathered around the elevators waiting for a ride. The doors opened, and they were swept inside, pressed together like colorful crayons squeezed into a too-small box.

From behind, Logan's arm circled her rib cage, his forearm brushing against the lower swell of her breast. She drew in a quick breath as he pulled her closer, and the continuing evidence of his arousal pressed against her buttocks. She twisted her hips, and knew the thrill of excitement when he groaned aloud.

"Easy, sweetheart," he whispered in her ear. "This is no time to get thrown out of the hotel."

She swallowed a laugh as the doors opened to the seventh floor.

A grown woman didn't run down hotel corridors. She wanted to. She wanted to drag Logan with her, into her room, into her bed. Into her life forever, if she could find a way.

They reached the door to her room. Shyly, not knowing quite what to do, suddenly losing confidence, she handed him her card key.

He slipped it into the slot, the light blinked green, and he pushed open the door.

Chapter Eleven

Logan's courage failed him.

From the doorway he caught sight of the double bed in Janice's room, the way the covers were turned down, the mint on the pillow. He was unable to move, unable to step into the room and take the one thing he wanted more than life itself.

She was vulnerable. He knew that. Knew, too, that she was willing. He'd seen it in her eyes. Heard it in the throaty sound of her voice.

But did he have a right to take advantage? For her, this had been an emotional journey. What could he offer her beyond a single night of pleasure? He couldn't ask Janice to share his life and risk the fire chief coming to her door a second time to announce she'd been widowed. That the red devil, the firefighter's greatest enemy, had taken another man from her.

That wouldn't be fair to her.

His conscience wrestled with his urge to pleasure her. She'd endured so much, had been so brave through it all, she deserved every bit of satisfaction a man could give a woman. The *right* man. He didn't qualify.

Her soft brown eyes questioned him. "Are you coming in?"

Switching tactics, his conscience warred with his hunger for her. "We'll have to leave by seven in the morning if you want to get home in time for school letting out. We wouldn't want to oversleep."

"We can leave a wake-up call."

"We'll have to pack, too."

"I didn't bring much with me."

Neither had he, and it was beginning to look like he'd left out a big chunk of good sense. "If you want breakfast, we'll have to—"

"No, after that big dinner, I won't be hungry for days."

"Right." He was running out of excuses. In the next three seconds he'd have to make the decision to walk into her room—or leave her standing there alone. Because he couldn't keep wrestling with his conscience. He'd lose.

She cocked her head to the side, and a bruised look appeared in her eyes, the sharp pain of rejection.

"I'm sorry," she said. "I should have realized. You had a long day driving up here, and you have to turn around and drive back tomorrow. And here I am preventing you from getting the rest you need. I'm not usually so thoughtless."

If she hadn't looked like a wounded animal who'd been betrayed, if she hadn't been concerned about his welfare instead of her own needs, Logan might not have stepped into her room. But he couldn't let her go on thinking he didn't want her. And once he crossed that threshold, the door swinging shut behind him, he had no choice but to pull her into his arms, crush his mouth to hers and savor the sweet taste he'd been craving all night.

After a moment's hesitation, of shock or surprise, her slender body molded against his. He felt big and awkward in comparison, and tender feelings rose up, flooding him with a potent need to protect her. To care for her as no other man ever had...or ever could.

He speared his fingers through the silken waves of her hair, cupping the back of her head, deepening their kiss. His tongue probed and explored. Timidly, hers responded with its own investigation.

By the time he broke the kiss, his heart was thundering in his chest. She was breathless, her cheeks flushed.

"If you're tired—"

"I'm not."

"It's been a long time since I—"

"For me, too." He slipped her jacket from her shoulders, revealing her ivy-green tank dress and baring her arms. "I want you, Janice. More than I've ever wanted any woman in my life."

"Ray used to complain because I—"

"There's no one named Ray in this room, sweetheart. It's just you and me." He found the zipper tab at the back of her dress, edged it down to her waist. With an easy tug, he stripped the dress away, revealing a beautiful woman in innocent white underwear. Before closing his mouth over her peaked nipple, he murmured, "You're perfect. Absolutely perfect."

A paroxysm of desire jolted Janice as his mouth claimed her breast. Even through the sheer fabric of her bra, moist heat seared her sensitive flesh, the friction of his caressing tongue sending rippling waves of hedonistic pleasure in all directions. Her knees turned weak and rubbery. She managed to keep standing only because her arms were linked around his shoulders.

Deep in her throat she made a sound that was half sob and half moan of pleasure.

She rubbed her cheek against his hair. Her fingers stroked across his back, feeling the flex of muscles, wanting to feel more. She tugged helplessly, trying to pull his shirt free of his pants.

"Your shirt...off."

With a low, rumbling growl, he gave up his grip on her breast in favor of shedding his shirt. Even while she relished the sight of his muscular chest, she missed the warmth of his mouth on her.

With little effort, he disposed of her underwear, tossing them carelessly aside, then lifted her off her feet, walking her backwards toward the bed. Together they fell, six inches of foam rubber catching them as she kicked off her heels. The crisp white sheet was cool on her back in contrast to the burning heat of his body touching hers and the raging fire that was building within her.

She felt no hesitation now. No inhibitions. His actions, the undisguised urgency of his need, his softly spoken words of praise, demanded a response, which she gave to him. Willingly. With all of her heart and soul.

The bedside light cast a soft glow around the room. Normally she might have been embarrassed, afraid he'd see the defects thirty years of life had left on her body. The extra pounds she'd gained. Fine white stretch marks, mementos of childbirth. But not now. Not with Logan.

In his eyes she saw approval, a reflected beauty she hadn't known existed. The joy of it, the validation, simply took her breath away.

When he finally rose above her, she lifted her hips to welcome his penetration with an eagerness that knew no bounds. The intimate collision of flesh on flesh thrilled and excited her further. As he claimed her, thrusting powerfully into her, she affirmed herself as a woman capable of giving love and being loved in return.

A moment later, she came apart, exploding into a thousand pieces, and cried out his name. He surged into her again. Through the passionate mist that enveloped her, she heard the echo of her own name on his lips.

It was like returning home after being exiled in some dry, desert land, and she found that here, at last, she was at peace.

DRAINED AND EXHAUSTED, Logan struggled back to some semblance of awareness. He lifted his weight off Janice, rolled to his side and pulled her closer. With a sigh, she snuggled against him.

As he had expected, she was the most totally giving, totally satisfying woman he'd ever known. In a thousand ways large and small, she'd aroused him with her simple innocence, her natural sensuality. No man could have found a better partner for a night—or for a lifetime.

But that wasn't a choice for Logan. Not as long as he remained a firefighter. That was too much to ask of any woman. His young wife had made that lesson clear to Logan years ago.

For Janice's sake, he mustn't forget it.

But deep in his gut he regretted that knowledge now more than he'd ever regretted anything in his life. To walk away from Janice when they returned to Paseo del Real tomorrow would take all the courage—all the decency—he could muster.

Tonight, he realized, would be his one and only chance to love her. Fighting against a sense of despair, he vowed it would be a night they would both remember.

When Logan roused her from a light doze with his kisses a few minutes later, Janice was momentarily torn between pleasure and the guilt that she could find such happiness in the arms of a man who was not her husband. She had a fleeting thought that a recent widow shouldn't be quite so wanton.

In another instant, that thought vanished, replaced by the swirling heat of Logan's tongue caressing her most intimate places and the lightning burst of desire that blazed through her once again.

THE MORNING following Logan's return from Las Vegas, Buttons fell into step beside him as he crossed the fire station yard.

"Hey, fella. How's it going?"

The dog's tail wagged an eager salute.

Mike Gables looked up from his task of stacking hose. "He's trying to tell you he's a daddy. Suzie had her puppies yesterday, four of 'em."

"Way to go, ol' man. You ought to be passing out cigars." Logan paused to give Buttons a congratulatory pat and tried not to feel envious of a dog because he had offspring and Logan didn't.

"They're the funniest-looking pups you've ever seen. Looks like they're going to have Suzie's mottled brown hair and Buttons's spots."

"Maddie will be tickled. She's looking forward to getting one of the puppies."

"Let her know, will you? They'll be weaned in about six weeks."

"Sure, I'll tell Janice." Except Logan knew he had to stay away from Janice and her kids. Far away.

When he'd dropped Janice off at home yesterday, he'd pleaded chores to be done, errands to be run. The truth was he hadn't dared linger with her because he never would have wanted to leave. Now that she was financially secure, now that some of the guilt for Ray's death had been lifted from his shoulders, he didn't have an excuse to stick around. It would just make things worse, making his leaving all the more difficult, for both of them.

So he'd practically left her on the doorstep, offering little more than lame excuses for his hasty departure.

Cowardly, that's what he'd been.

But how the hell could he be honest with her? As long as he was a firefighter, as long as he fought smoke and flames and the red devil, he'd never marry. Janice deserved better than a one-night stand, but that's all he could give her. Because that's how much he loved her.

He snatched up a mop, filled a bucket with soapy water and began to swab down the bay floor. The morning's PT session hadn't lessened his frustration. Maybe scrubbing floors would.

"Hey, Strong! You trying to wear away that concrete or trying out for a new Olympic sport?"

With a scowl, Logan turned to Danny Sullivan, who was polishing the connectors on Engine 62. He'd recently transferred in from Station Three and had already promised to bring home the highest bid at the Bachelor Auction next year. With his smooth Irish tongue and a twinkle in his blue eyes that drove women crazy, he was likely to do it, too.

"I'm cleaning up the mess you and your engine company left, okay?"

"Oh, woman troubles, huh?" Danny gave him a knowing grin.

Logan didn't want any part of his kidding. "Shove it, Sullivan." With a swipe of his mop, he worked on an imaginary grease stain and wished he could as easily whisk away his errant thoughts.

The afternoon went as miserably as the morning

had. To distract himself he concocted a three-cheese vegetable lasagna for dinner using eggplant and every spice he could find in the cupboard. He had no idea how it would taste.

Emma Jean came strolling in while it was cooking, her jewelry jingling in a distracting off-key way with every step.

"Something sure smells good up here." She sniffed the air. "Ahh. Heaven. I could use a man around the house who cooks. Logan, will you marry me?"

"No," he groused.

Her dark brows shot up. "Oh-oh. Woman trouble, huh?"

He slammed down the serving spoon he'd pulled from the kitchen drawer. "Why does everyone think I've got woman troubles all of a sudden? Maybe I'm just worried about the oral exam tomorrow. Wouldn't that make sense, too?" Not that he'd given the exam much thought, despite how important the promotion was to him. He'd been too wrapped up in thoughts of Janice—and desperately trying not to think about her at all.

Emma Jean leaned on the counter. "Nope. Your aura is definitely chartreuse with red streaks running through it. That's woman trouble, if I ever saw it."

"Chartr—" he sputtered. "My aura is none of your—"

"I'm psychic. You know that. I can see all kinds of things."

He bent down so they were virtually nose-to-nose

across the counter. He gritted his teeth. "Shouldn't you be downstairs answering 911 calls?"

"I'm on my break."

"Take your break somewhere else, Emma Jean."

Straightening, she took a step back. "You don't have to worry, Logan. I can pretty well see—"

"Don't see, don't look. No one's interested in your psycho-babble."

"Well," she huffed, sending her jewelry tinkling again. "If that's how you feel—" Whirling, she marched out of the upstairs recreation room. Her feet clattered on the stairs, the tinny sound of her bracelets knocking together discordantly.

The few firefighters hanging around gave Logan a puzzled look.

He hung his head and speared his fingers through his hair. Emma Jean hadn't deserved his wrath. Just as Janice deserved better than Logan could give.

With a determined stride, he headed off after Emma Jean to apologize.

"So tell me how Las Vegas was…and your gentleman friend?" Debbie, Janice's neighbor, waggled her eyebrows. "Was he wonderful?"

More than that, Janice thought, but she was still upset and confused by the way Logan had left her yesterday. Not even a goodbye kiss. Surely a kiss wouldn't have taken that much time away from the errands he'd had to run.

"I accomplished what I set out to do," she responded, rather primly. "The casino has written off

Ray's gambling debts, which is a terrific load off my shoulders."

"That's wonderful, and I know you must feel relieved." She grinned. "But what about *him?*"

Janice didn't need her friend to define who she meant by *him.*

She sat down at the end of her couch and folded her legs beneath her. The children were upstairs, Kevin doing his homework, Maddie in bed, though probably not yet asleep. This had been the first time she and Debbie had had a chance to talk since Janice's return from Vegas yesterday. And the fact was, Janice needed someone to talk to.

"His name is Logan—Logan Strong—one of Ray's fellow firefighters on the ladder truck. He felt like it was his fault that Ray died."

"You mean he was responsible—"

"No, not really." Janice went on to describe what she'd learned in Las Vegas, including meeting Ray's girlfriend and Christie's views of Ray's state of mind that fateful morning.

Debbie nodded from time to time and made understanding noises, even as her eyes widened at the news that Ray had been unfaithful.

"The unseen victim here," Janice concluded, "beyond me and my children, was Logan. He was carrying around a lot of guilt over what happened. I think he still blames himself."

"A guilty conscience sure can play havoc on a man," Debbie agreed.

But did a guilty conscience result in an incredible

night of lovemaking? Janice didn't know. She only wished he'd called her today. She would have felt much better if he had.

"Well, I gotta go." Debbie levered herself up from the chair. "I'm sure one way or the other, things will work out for you. But I'm sure going to miss you when you move."

"Thanks." She gave her friend a hug. "I'll miss you, too. And so will the kids."

"Ha! They'll only miss my swimming pool."

Silently agreeing that was probably all too true, Janice showed her friend to the door, then returned to the kitchen, intending to clean up the dishes. Instead, she found her son standing in the middle of the room, his expression a mixture of horror and dismay.

"What's wrong, Kevin?"

"D-dad." His voice broke. "Did Logan kill my d-dad?"

"Oh, my heavens, no!" She went to her son, wanting to hold him, reassure him, but the boy slipped away. Dear God! What had he heard? How *much* had he heard?

"Was it Logan's fault Dad died, Mom? Was it?"

"No, honey. There wasn't anything Logan could do." How could she tell her son his father *wanted* to die? Was so distressed by his own failings that he'd walked into that inferno without any intention of coming back? And how could she possibly know that for sure? "Being a firefighter is a dangerous—"

"No! I heard you and Debbie talking. It was Logan's fault." The desperation in the boy's eyes, his rising voice, spoke of panic and confusion. "I liked him, Mom. I thought Logan was cool. And he...he's your boyfriend, isn't he?"

"Kevin, that's not your—"

"He's your boyfriend and...and he killed my dad!" Spinning around, Kevin burst out of the back door.

"Wait!" Appalled. Embarrassed. Guilty as sin, she ran after him.

He didn't stop. Instead, he jumped onto his bicycle. Dust flew up from beneath the tires as he pedaled out of the driveway. A car honked and tires squealed as a passing motorist barely missed colliding with her son.

Janice's heart leaped into her throat. "Kevin! Be careful!"

He ignored her. There was no way Janice could catch up with her son. He was too strong, too fast, for her to catch him on foot. Even if she followed him in the van, he wouldn't come back willingly. He'd still be fighting her.

And fighting his confusion over loyalty to his father, a man so often absent from his life, and his newer feelings for Logan. Not entirely unlike the way Janice was still wrestling with her own confused loyalties.

She tried not to panic, tried not to overreact. Her son knew the area. He wouldn't go far. Their neighborhood was safe—or as safe as any these days. She vacillated about what to do. Race after him in the van, leaving Maddie alone in the house? Or wait, having faith her son would find his own way back home when it was time?

Her life felt so out of control she didn't know what

to do. She couldn't lose Kevin, not her baby who'd grown so tall and strong.

In her entire life, she'd never been so confused about her best course of action.

A dreadful combination of fear and anger churned through her stomach.

Closing her eyes, she prayed for guidance.

THE PHONE in the rec room at the station house rang just before the eight o'clock shift change the next morning.

"Strong!" Jay Tolliver shouted down the hallway to the sleeping quarters. "Phone!"

Dread kicked Logan in the gut. He rarely got calls at the station. For a moment all he could think was that something had happened to his father. Or to his brother in Merced.

"Hustle it up, Strong. It's a woman. Sounds like a *pretty* woman to me."

Janice? Dropping his duffel on the bed, he jogged down the hallway and snatched the phone from Jay's hand.

"Strong here."

"Logan, have you seen Kevin?"

It was Janice's voice all right, but Logan had trouble processing her question. He'd been expecting something else. Hoping for words he shouldn't be waiting to hear.

"Kevin?" he echoed.

"He hasn't been home all night. He ran away. On his bike. I've been looking for him everywhere."

"Why did he run away? What happened?"

"He…he heard me talking to Debbie. He misunderstood. He th-thinks you were responsible for Ray's death."

Logan swore under his breath. This was his worst nightmare, having a boy he cared about believing Logan was responsible for his father's death. "Have you called the police?"

"They've been looking for him since last night. There hasn't been a single sign of him. I was hoping—" Her voice caught on a sob. "I thought maybe he'd come by the station house. To see you."

"I haven't seen him." He tried to think like a kid. If the boy hadn't come here, where would Kevin go? "Maybe the cemetery. If he's that upset—"

"I drove out there last night and again this morning. No one has seen him. The caretaker—"

"He has to be someplace. With a friend?"

"I've called everyone I can think of." Her voice was excited. High pitched. On the verge of panic. "Maybe…maybe he went out to the lake. He liked rowing your boat. It's a long way but maybe… Logan, I'm so afraid—"

"I know, Jan. I know." He checked his watch. "I'm off the clock as of now. The A-shift crew is all here. I'll get out to the lake as fast as I can." And break every speeding law doing it, if he had to.

"You'll let me know? One way or the other?"

"I'll call." Leaning his forehead against the wall, he closed his eyes, picturing Janice and feeling her desperation. "We'll find him, Jan. He's a good boy.

Smart. He can take care of himself. You'll have him home in no time."

"Hurry, Logan. Please. I'm going crazy. I don't know where else to turn."

"You did the right thing by calling me."

After a moment's hesitation, she said, "There's something else, something you aren't going to like." She paused again. "He accused us of having a relationship—you being my boyfriend. I'm sorry. I didn't want him to know."

"I'll find him, Jan. I'll explain." Like hell he would. How could any man explain to a kid that he was sleeping with the boy's mother? As far as Kevin was concerned, Logan had crossed a line that was worse than killing his father.

He'd destroyed the boy's image of his mother.

Logan didn't waste any time getting to his car. Despite the morning rush hour, traffic out of the city was light. He went through signals on the red and cut a corner through a gas station when he got stuck behind a slow truck. If the cops spotted him, so be it. He'd argue the ticket later.

Breathless, his heart pounding as if he'd run a marathon, he arrived at his house. Dust was still billowing up behind his car when he parked and jumped out.

Not wanting to frighten Kevin or drive him into hiding—if he was there—Logan forced himself to calm down. To take it slow as he rounded the house to the lake side.

Disappointment arced through him when he spotted the rowboat still upside down on the dock, the oars stacked beside it. In a kid's mind, it would have made sense to have headed here, to the lake, and to seek refuge out on the isolated island.

Except Kevin had to hate Logan now. *He'd killed his father.* Or that's what the boy believed. *And was having an affair with his mother.*

He circled the house. No sign of a bike or Kevin. No evidence of the boy inside either. Nothing had been disturbed, not even the unopened half gallon of milk in the refrigerator.

Logan picked up the phone and dialed Janice's number.

"He's not here," Logan said when she answered. "Have you had any word?"

"No. Nothing. Oh, God, Logan, what am I going to do?"

"Wait right where you are. I'm on my way."

Chapter Twelve

She shoved open the screen door before he reached the steps, and then she was on the porch, emotion etched in her heart-shaped face. Lines of worry fanned out from her red-rimmed eyes, making them look overly large and bruised with fatigue. Deep grooves creased her forehead. Her hair was disheveled. She wore no makeup. Her clothes looked as if she'd slept in them but Logan suspected she hadn't closed her eyes all night.

He had never seen a woman more beautiful…or more exposed.

Taking her in his arms, Logan held her because that was the only thing he could think to do. He wanted to do more. Ease her pain. Magically produce her son from the back seat of his car. Tell her the boy had meant it as a joke. He hadn't really run away.

That she didn't have to worry.

But there was no way he or anyone else could erase a mother's fears until her son was safely back home.

She trembled against him, and he brushed a kiss to the top of her head.

"No news?" he asked, though the answer was obvious.

She shook her head. "I keep thinking he'll come pedaling his bike up the street any minute, and I'll be able to let him know what a dumb stunt he pulled by running away. But he hasn't come and it's been so long. Last night, I never thought—" The effort it took for her not to cry, not to break down, radiated in tense waves from her slender body.

"Let's go inside." Keeping one arm around her, he led her back into the house. "Where's Maddie?"

"I had Debbie take her to school. I thought it would be easier if—" Her breath caught on a near sob. "The police said for me to stay here in case, but I just can't—" Words seemed to escape her. "They're keeping an eye out for him."

"Good. Now, have you eaten?"

She looked puzzled by his question as if eating was an exotic activity she'd never experienced. "No. I don't think I could swallow—"

"You need to keep up your strength. I'll scramble you some eggs."

"You don't have to—"

"Yeah, I do." He urged her to sit on a stool at the breakfast counter and went to work preparing a meal, to keep himself busy, to keep his own fears under control.

She'd already begun packing her household goods for the move and there were boxes stacked everywhere, but he found a frying pan in the cupboard, butter and eggs in the refrigerator.

"After I called you, I remembered you have your oral exam today. You don't want to miss—"

"I'm here for as long as you need me. Until I know the boy is safe, I probably couldn't give a coherent response to any question, much less the technical ones they'd ask."

"Kevin running away isn't your fault. He's just a boy. He doesn't understand."

"About Ray—or you?"

"Both."

"A boy puts his mother on a pedestal. Kevin thinks I not only killed his father, I pulled that pedestal out from under you, too. He connects the two. It may take him a long time to forgive either of us."

"I fell off that pedestal years ago."

Something in her tone, the echo of a long-held pain, made Logan look up from the eggs he'd cracked into the pan.

She twisted her hands together on the countertop. "My parents thought I was perfect. Their sweet little girl who could do no wrong. And then I got pregnant with Kevin."

"You weren't married." It wasn't a question. Logan knew the answer.

"Ray hadn't intended to get me pregnant. He'd taken precautions. Then, when my parents virtually disowned me…" She fiddled with the salt shaker sitting on the counter, her fingers trembling. "All along I think Ray felt trapped. He tried to do the right thing, and for a while it worked. I think he may have actually fallen in love with Christie, and then he was trapped between his gambling debts and whatever obligation he felt to us. He wasn't a bad man. We just weren't right for each other.''

That didn't excuse a man for being unfaithful or for turning his back on his family. Or for the emotional damage he'd done to his wife, making her believe she wasn't competent, wasn't beautiful. For that, if nothing else, Ray had earned Logan's contempt.

Forcefully controlling a flare of anger, Logan stirred the eggs and slipped a piece of bread into the toaster. ''What happened ten years ago doesn't mean you were a bad woman then—or now.''

She looked at him steadily. ''But how do I explain it to Kevin?''

''He loves you. You'll find a way.'' Logan was hardly an expert on child rearing but he did know, given enough time, Kevin would figure out that his mother deserved his respect no matter what she'd done in the past. And he'd be a better man because of it. Meanwhile, Logan would have to make sure he kept his distance from Janice, not adding fuel to the fire.

But keeping his distance would come later, after Kevin was back home.

He slid the plate of eggs and toast onto the counter in front of Janice. ''Eat,'' he ordered. ''When Kevin shows up, I don't want you to faint from hunger.''

Unable to watch her toying with her food, Logan switched on the TV in the corner of the kitchen, as much to add some noise to the oppressive quiet of the house as to see if there was any news. He turned to the local channel.

Across the top of the screen, red letters announced Breaking News, and there was a picture of a scene taken from a helicopter.

"—the fire apparently started as a result of an out-of-control delivery truck crashing through the wire fence. This particular warehouse at the corner of Broadway and First Street was the site of a fatality only months ago when Firefighter Raymond Gainer lost his life fighting another blaze," the announcer said. "In the interim, city officials have been arguing with the owners of the property, trying to determine who should be responsible for tearing down the charred remains of the building. The impasse—"

Logan stopped listening. He turned to Janice and their eyes met. In that instant, they both knew Kevin was inside that building. A gut feeling. The logic unassailable. That's where a boy would go to mourn the loss of his father.

Without a word, Logan raced toward the front door and out to his car.

"I'm going with you!" Janice shouted.

"You'll be in the way. Stay here!"

She reached the Mustang at almost the same moment he did and yanked open the passenger door. "I'm not going to lose a husband *and* a son to that damn building. I'm going with you."

Logan didn't have time to argue.

He might not have a siren on his Mustang, but he sure as hell had a horn. He laid on it all the way into town, ignoring traffic lights and stop signs, weaving through traffic like an Indy race driver set on overtaking the competition.

He pulled up at the scene, quickly assessing the situation as he got out of the car. Four engine companies, two ladder trucks. They were laying water on the fire from the perimeter. But nobody was going inside.

If the fire crews had a choice, they wanted what was left of the building to burn to the ground. Nobody wanted to risk the life of another firefighter in the same derelict building. They'd rather save the city some money.

He'd never changed out of his uniform that morning, which got him through the police barricades. Behind him, he heard Janice loudly complaining the cops wouldn't let her follow him to the fire. He was thankful for that.

He spotted a friend of his father's from Station Four standing by the pumper monitoring the flow of water.

"Gimme your jacket, Lucas."

"Huh? Logan? Whataya—"

"There's a kid in there. Ray Gainer's boy. I'm going in after him."

"No way, man."

"You can't stop me. I'm either going in with your gear on, or I'm going in bare-faced. If that happens, I probably won't come out alive."

"I'll tell the battalion chief—"

"There's no time." Logan practically wrenched the guy's helmet from his head, and he gave up his turnout coat a minute later. "Your breathing apparatus, too, man."

An old-timer who'd been in the department since Logan's father's days, Lucas said, "Your dad is gonna kill me. Let me go in with you."

"No." He wouldn't risk anyone else's life on what could already be a lost cause. "But see that the guys cover me as I go inside."

"It's a good fire, youngster. Hot."

He knew that. Black smoke was still billowing out of the broken windows of the building. The only place that Kevin could be and still survive was at the far end, the section that had been left undamaged from the last fire. The fire that had killed the boy's father.

Squeezing through an opening in the wire fence, Logan headed in that direction.

A POLICE OFFICER built like a brick wall had snared Janice. She tried to shove past him but it was no good. He wouldn't let her go.

"Ma'am, you have to stay behind the yellow tape."

"You don't understand. My son's in there." And the man she loved was going after him.

"The firefighters are in charge, ma'am. You'll have to wait here."

"Don't you see? They aren't doing *anything*. They're going to let it burn to the ground this time."

"I'm sorry, ma'am." He forcibly restrained her.

"Let me go!" she screamed, her struggles useless. "Oh, God…"

Frantically, she looked around. Streams of water poured on the flames with little effect. Choking smoke tumbled from the windows like ugly dark marshmallows, and she watched as a single firefighter jogged toward the entrance.

"Logan!" she screamed. His name ripped from her throat, but she was helpless to stop him. As helpless as he had been to stop Ray from going to his death once the decision had been made.

But Janice couldn't give up. Not yet. Not until there was no other choice. Too much was at stake.

Nearby, the fire chief's red car rolled to a stop. In a frenzy of hope and determination, Janice broke free of the police officer.

"Chief Gray, my son's in there!"

Startled, the chief turned to her. "Janice, what are you—"

"I think my son's in the warehouse. Logan's gone after him. Please, chief, do something. I don't want to lose—"

Before she'd finished the thought, the chief was speaking into his Handie Talkie. Firefighters had already begun to move, making their way closer to the building, readjusting the spray of water, following Logan into the conflagration with a two-inch hose.

Janice covered her mouth to prevent another scream. She *couldn't* lose both her son and the man she loved to the same fire. God wouldn't be that cruel.

SWEAT DRIPPED DOWN Logan's face inside his helmet and slid along his neck. Behind him, the fire roared like a freight train, black smoke swirling towards him. Clean air swept in and out of his lungs as he breathed through the mouthpiece, drawing deeply. Calmly. Despite the thudding of his heart. Without bunker pants, the heat from the fire seeped through his uniform, scalding his legs.

He kept on moving. Searching.

Logan hadn't been able to save Ray Gainer.

This time would be different. He wouldn't give up until he found Kevin. Or died trying. For Janice's sake. And his own.

There was no way to know if the boy had stayed on the ground floor or gone up the ancient, wobbly stairs. So Logan searched methodically, aware of the smoke, his own heavy breathing, and the fear that was gnawing in his gut.

Smoke was the deadliest killer of them all.

In one corner of the second floor he found some bedding, a jumble of blankets that looked as if they'd been turned into a rat's nest. He poked at the debris with his foot...and touched something solid.

Kneeling, he jerked the blankets aside. Beneath the mess, Kevin was curled into a ball, an innocent child, his dirt-streaked face stained by tears.

Logan touched the boy's neck, found a pulse, weak but steady, his respirations slow and shallow. He pulled his mouthpiece out of his mouth and slipped it into Kevin's.

"Breathe, son. Don't check out on me. You don't want to break your mother's heart."

He hefted the boy in his arms, the effort costing him a deep breath, and he coughed. When he turned, he realized the smoke and flames had caught up with him, blocking his way back to the stairs. Flares of orange and red tongued the railing and licked across the steps, the dry wood drawing in the fire as though thirsty for its touch.

The only windows on this floor were too high and too small to crawl through, the burning stairs their only route of escape.

Putting the boy down again, Logan shrugged off his breathing apparatus and took off his jacket, wrapping it protectively around Kevin. Knowing Kevin wouldn't have a chance if he passed out, Logan strapped on the breathing tanks again, took a deep breath of clear air, and, with the boy in his arms, headed for the stairs.

He pictured Janice waiting for him on the other side of the flames and smoke, and he held that image as he descended into hell.

Chapter Thirteen

The wait was interminable.

More engine companies arrived, sirens wailing. Two ambulances screamed onto the scene. The water cannon on the ladder truck delivered an arching column of water onto the warehouse. The sun caught the spray, turning it into a rainbow of color, but beneath the fleeting beauty deadly black smoke snaked out around the derelict building.

Janice clung to the roof of the chief's vehicle while behind her gawking civilians jostled together and pressed against the police line.

Holding her breath, paralyzed with fear, she *willed* Logan to reappear with her son. She would not—*could not*—accept that they were lost in the fiery inferno. Surely her love was powerful enough to guide them to safety.

A cheer went up on the far side of the warehouse.

Unable to stand waiting a moment longer, she ducked beneath the yellow tape and dashed past the distracted police officer toward clamoring cheers.

Bedlam reigned as firefighters converged on a single figure walking away from the building.

Janice's heart faltered. *Logan!* But where was her son? Dear Lord, where was Kevin?

Then she saw the bundle Logan carried in his arms, something wrapped in a fire jacket. Motionless. A dead weight.

Fear nearly drove her to her knees. "Kevin!" She raced forward. Nothing, no one, could stop her from reaching her baby. Her first-born.

Strong hands restrained her before she could snatch her son from Logan's embrace.

"He's breathing," Logan said. Soot streaked his face, but beneath the grime his dimple appeared. "He's going to be okay."

Those were the most beautiful words Janice had ever heard.

Then Logan dropped to his knees, his eyes rolled up until only the whites showed, and he passed out.

THE NURSE bustled into the curtained cubicle with a clipboard in her hand. A brassy blonde with a quick smile and a no-nonsense attitude, her name tag read Adrian Goodfellow, but Janice had heard the doctors call her Addy.

"When you have a chance, Mrs. Gainer, Admissions would like you to fill out these forms. You know how insurance companies can be."

"Of course." Reluctantly, Janice relinquished her grip on Kevin's hand. The Emergency Room doctors had poked and prodded at her son, and except for some mild smoke inhalation—which had rendered him temporarily unconscious—and singed hair, they had declared him fit. Falling asleep under that heap of blankets had trapped enough air with him to save him until Logan had arrived.

In contrast, she wasn't sure she'd ever recover from the trauma of watching Logan walk into that burning building alone and then, what seemed like hours later, seeing him reappear with her unconscious son in his arms. And then collapse at her feet. The memory still had the power to stall her heartbeat, and she shuddered.

"Can I get you anything?" the nurse asked, concerned.

"I'm fine, really." If only she could stop shaking on the inside. "What about Logan—the firefighter who—"

"Our local hero?" Addy grinned broadly. "They don't make 'em any stronger or sweeter than Logan Strong, or braver as it turns out. Your boy here was darn lucky Logan came along."

Kevin looked embarrassed.

"Yes, I know," Janice said, "but I haven't seen him since they brought him into emergency. Was he seriously hurt?"

"Nope. A little singed around the edges, but he's a lucky fellow, too. Seems like some smart woman ought to latch onto the man before he takes one too many risks." She waggled her eyebrows and shook her head. "Real pity after all this time he hasn't given me a tumble, and not for my lack of trying, either."

Janice didn't know quite how to respond to Addy's comment, so she simply nodded sympathetically.

"The doctor admitted him for observation if you're interested in dropping by his room upstairs when you're done here."

"Yes, we'd like to do that."

Winking, Addy said, "Who knows, maybe you'll be the one to latch onto the man. I hear he's a great cook." With that, the nurse left them alone.

Kevin finally found his voice. "I guess I really screwed up, huh?" His face was still dirty, his voice husky, he smelled of smoke, and Janice's heart filled once again with relief and love.

"Running away is never the answer to any problem," she said. It hadn't been the answer for Kevin's father any more than it had been for his son.

"No, I mean this is gonna cost you, isn't it?"

She stroked his dark, sweat-sticky hair. "Don't worry. We'll manage. Besides, you're worth every penny and more. Don't you ever forget that. I love you, Kevin."

"Yeah." He didn't hold her gaze.

Her stomach knotted on the fear that while Kevin was alive, she'd lost her son's love and respect. She needed to get that back, or at least resolve some of the issues that had so troubled him. "Let's talk about why you ran away."

"Can't we just go home, Mom? I'm hungry."

"First, I want you to understand it wasn't Logan's fault your father died. We'll never know for sure what happened that day." And she felt no need to share her suspicion that Ray had effectively given up and walked across that roof knowing he'd never come back. "But I am sure his last thoughts were about his family—you and me and Maddie. There was nothing Logan could have said or done that would have saved your father's life, or he would have done it."

"He saved me, didn't he?"

"He did. And he could have died trying." She was anxious to see for herself that Logan was all right and thank him for risking his own life to save her son.

"But you and him, I mean, it just doesn't seem right, you know? Like, Dad hasn't been dead that long."

This part was more difficult to explain to a nine-year-old, or to herself, for that matter. Under the circumstances she didn't feel she could reveal that she loved Logan. Certainly not until she knew whether he returned her feelings. And given Kevin's fragile understanding of the situation, her revelations might have to wait for a long time.

"Could you just trust me on this, Kevin? Nothing Logan or I have done takes away from the fact that I love you very much. Your father did, too. And Maddie. That's what you need to focus on the next time you get upset with me about anything."

He studied her with serious eyes much like his father's. "Even when you make me take out the trash?"

"Even then." She smiled, sensing her son would be all right. He might not understand everything that had happened in the past two months but he was willing to give her some slack.

She tugged him to a sitting position on the Emergency Room gurney. "How 'bout we go see Logan? I think we owe him our thanks."

LOGAN HAD FLUIDS flowing into his arm via an IV, his hands were swathed in gauze and his lower legs stung like crazy, but he was okay. Based on the doctor's reports, so was Kevin. Logan couldn't ask for more than that.

Beside his bed, Logan's father stood, looking frail and worried.

"I thought I taught you not to be a hero," he said. The bright light of parental distress glistened in his eyes. "Firefighting's a team effort, not a solo sport."

"Sorry, Dad. At the time, it seemed like the right thing to do." It still did, as far as Logan was concerned, and he'd do it all over again if faced with the same decision.

"Your mother would shoot me if you got seriously hurt on the job. I always told her fighting fires was lots safer than being an accountant." His lips twitched. "All those numbers would drive me crazy and I'd probably jump out the window."

Logan had heard the story a thousand times, but he still smiled. "Where'd she go?" His mother had been in the room, then had vanished while he'd been talking to his father.

"She claimed she was going to go see Mrs. Linfield, who's here for a hip replacement. Truth to tell, I think it was hard for your mother to see you in a hospital bed. Women are like that. They stand up just fine till the excitement's all over, then they fall apart.''

Gripping the guard rail, Logan shifted his position on the bed. "Is that how she was when you fought fires?''

"Claimed she never gave me a thought while I was on duty. She was too busy raising you boys. But she was right there at the front door when I came off my shift.'' He pulled a chair up beside the bed and sat down.

"Torie hated me being a firefighter.''

"I remember. But every woman's different, son. I'm not sure you should base the whole rest of your life on what your ex-wife told you.''

"Maybe not. But I can see being a firefighter's wife isn't all fun and games.'' Even his mother, who Logan had thought coped well with the danger of her husband's job, had had her moments of anxiety. Logan was right not to pursue Janice for the same reason.

"Your mother and I have had a good life together. I don't think she'd have traded it to marry a garage mechanic or some such.''

No, but his mother hadn't lost her husband to the job. Janice had. No woman in her right mind would want to take that risk again.

As if thinking about Janice made her materialize, she appeared in the doorway. With a quiet gasp, she stepped into the room.

"They told me you weren't badly hurt! What's all this?'' She made a vague sweep of her hand to include

Logan's IV and his bandages, and she got a fearful look in her eyes.

Logan hastened to reassure her. "I'm not hurt, honest. A few second-degree burns and a lot less hair on my legs than I used to have, which only means I won't look so good in my kilt for a while."

She didn't look convinced or amused. "What about that IV?"

"It's only a precaution to be sure my fluids are okay." He gestured for her to come closer. "I want you to meet my father, Harry Strong. Dad, this is Janice Gainer."

With visible effort, she pulled her attention away from Logan and shook his father's hand. "And this young man—" she beckoned Kevin into the room "—is why your son is in that hospital bed. Kevin?"

The boy kept his head down and his hands stuffed in his pockets. "I'm sorry, Logan," he mumbled. He'd obviously been prompted by his mother to apologize for the trouble he'd caused. It was equally clear he wasn't sure about his feelings for Logan. "I didn't mean for you to get hurt."

"It's okay, Kevin. I'm just glad we both got out of there without much more than singed eyebrows to show for it."

Janice slid her arm around the boy's shoulders. "I'm afraid, Mr. Strong, that my son's adventure caused Logan to miss his oral exam, too. I know how much Logan wanted to get that promotion."

Harry Strong rested his hand on Logan's arm. "I'd say my son had his priorities in order. Your son's life is far more important than any promotion, or any job, for that matter. I'm very proud of my boy.''

A lump formed in Logan's throat. Once he'd heard that Kevin had run away, he hadn't given the oral exam another thought. And he was glad his father felt he'd made the right decision. There'd be other testing cycles, other chances for promotion. They just might not come soon enough for his father to pin a new engineer's shield on Logan's shirt.

Pulling himself to his feet, Logan's father spoke to Kevin. ''I don't know about you, young man, but hanging around a hospital makes me thirsty. Could you use a canned drink? I'm buying.''

The boy shrugged. ''Sure, I guess.''

''Good. Then let's have a look-see what they've got down the hall.'' Moving slowly, he looped his arm over the boy's shoulder both for support and reassurance. ''You play any sports, young man?'' he asked as the two of them walked out into the hallway, turning toward the family waiting room.

Janice smiled when they were out of sight. ''Your father's very nice.''

''Perceptive, too. He must have figured we'd want a minute alone.''

She lingered at the foot of his bed. ''You're sure you're going to be all right? Your hands—''

''I'll maybe milk a week or two on disability, then I'll be back on the job. I was very lucky. So was Kevin.''

''He *is* sorry he put you both at risk. I don't think he'll be running away again anytime soon.''

"I sure hope not, for all our sakes." Sensing her discomfort, he forced a smile.

Her fingers moved uneasily along the foot board of his bed, and she picked up a towel that had been left there, folding it carefully, then laying it back down again. Logan knew she had something to say and couldn't find the words.

"It's okay, Jan," he said softly.

She looked up. "It's Kevin. He's still confused—about us, I mean. And his father. I think it would be better if, for now, at least, that we not—"

"—see each other," he finished for her. Even though he'd known this was coming, knew it was the right thing to do, the words seared him more painfully than third-degree burns would. "I understand, Jan. Your family comes first."

She hesitated again. Her eyes glistened with unshed tears, her chin trembled. "I'll never be able to thank you enough. For everything."

He wanted her to go before he pleaded with her to stay. Before he forgot he couldn't give her what she needed.

Abruptly, she whirled and ran out the door.

Logan's whispered good-bye locked in his throat.

BETWEEN CARING for her son, making sure Maddie was reassured about her brother, and worrying about Logan, Janice had a fretful night.

Despite his father's reassurances, she felt badly that Logan's heroics had cost him a chance for promotion. At least she could clear the air with Chief Gray about what had happened to Ray, remove any doubts that Logan had been responsible for her husband's death.

After dropping the children at school the next morning, she drove to the fire station.

Chief Gray stood as she entered his office. "Mrs. Gainer. How's your boy?"

"No worse for wear, thanks to Logan and your men."

The chief, always the image of spit-and-polish in his uniform, ushered her to a chair. "It's too little, too late, I know, but the city has bulldozers out on the warehouse site this morning tearing down what's left of the building."

"At least no one else will be hurt there."

"Should have been done years ago." He leaned back on the edge of his desk, his expression friendly. "Now, what can I do for you?"

"It's about Logan. I'm afraid others may blame him for Ray's death, and I wanted you to know the truth." She proceeded to relate what she'd learned in Las Vegas, including telling him about Ray's gambling debts and infidelity, and how his death might well have been suicide. She had trouble meeting the chief's sympathetic gaze. But Logan deserved her honesty.

The chief gave her shoulder a paternal squeeze when she finished.

"I'm sorry about your husband, and I have been worried about Strong. He's always been one of our best men. Lately, though, he's set himself apart from the others. It made me question whether he was ready for promotion."

"He felt so guilty."

"Rest assured, none of us blamed him. He's so darn conscientious, though, I can see how he'd be harder on himself than anyone else would be."

"I feel like my family has already cost him a promotion because he missed the oral exam. I didn't want there to be any lingering question later on that Logan could have prevented Ray's death."

"I appreciate how difficult a time you've had lately and how hard it was for you to tell me all that you have." He straightened. "As far as I'm concerned, both your husband and Logan Strong are heroes. I'll make sure the men understand that, too."

He took her hand as she stood, and Janice was grateful there was no need for her to speak. The emotions crowding in her throat would have made it impossible to utter a sound.

HIS FIRST DAY back at work, Logan climbed the stairs to the station's living quarters. There'd been plenty of cars in the employee parking lot. But downstairs it had been eerily quiet. Nobody around the fire trucks, the offices deserted.

Maybe there was a special training session going on he hadn't heard about.

He opened the door to the rec room.

"Hail the returning hero!" chorused a whole room full of firefighters and support staff. A huge paper banner was draped across the room with the words *Welcome Back* printed in red, white and blue stripes. Logan was stunned and momentarily speechless as well as secretly pleased.

He ducked under the banner. "Aw, come on, guys. Isn't that a bit much?"

"It would be," Diaz piped up, "except we're all sick of Tolliver's cooking."

"Yeah, all he knows how to fix is noodles 'n' nothing," Gables complained.

"We're trying to make you feel so good about coming back that you'll do your linguini for us," Diaz confessed.

"I gave it a try one night," Greg Turrick said, "and they told me to go back to my singing."

"It must have been really bad if they were willing to suffer through your lonesome cowboy routine," Logan countered.

The whole room burst into laughter at that, and Logan suddenly felt more at home than he had in the past two weeks moping around his own house. He'd missed Janice and her kids more than he'd thought possible.

But he hadn't realized how much he'd missed the camaraderie of the fire station, too. The brotherhood. Jay Tolliver and Mike Gables had dropped by the house last week and told him they all understood he wasn't to blame for Ray's death, which had lifted another weight from Logan's shoulders. Being a firefighter meant a hell of a lot more than simply drawing a paycheck.

"Tell you what, gentlemen," he said, grinning. "If you volunteer to handle the clean-up, I'll do clam linguini. *And* I'll throw in dessert, too. Homemade apple pie.''

They all cheered.

Dodging friendly back slaps and a good many verbal jabs about lazing around on his days off, Logan worked his way down the hall to his sleeping quarters. He dropped his duffel on the bed and took a deep breath.

It was good to be back.

JANICE WALKED into Kim's office, easing her way around a stack of magazines to the chair in front of her boss's desk.

''What's up?'' Kim asked, lifting her head from the script she'd been working on.

''How do you feel about insurance for seniors to cover veterinary expenses?''

''I'd rather have them treated by MDs,'' Kim said, straight-faced.

Grinning, Janice passed Kim an article she'd downloaded from the Internet. She'd been on the job a little over a week and she was really getting the hang of the computer and searching out topics that would work for Kim's late-night talk show.

''Seems a congressman from Florida has learned that elderly people with pets live longer on average than those who don't. So he's proposing—''

Kim held up her hand. ''Don't tell me. A cat in every household.''

''Something like that. He's concluded that some seniors don't have pets because of the expense, so he wants Social Security to cover the cost of regular checkups for the seniors' pets.''

''Seniors who just happen to make up a majority of his constituency?''

''That would be my guess.''

Twisting her lips into a wry smile, Kim said, ''When I asked you to find a topic that fit in with National Pet Month, I had no idea. Obviously you have talents I haven't yet plumbed.''

Janice basked in her praise. She couldn't imagine a more perfect job, one she would enjoy so much. That she spent her nights missing Logan couldn't be helped. For now, it was better she focus on Kevin and Maddie, and settling into their new townhouse. Soon they'd be adding a new resident to their household—Buttons's offspring. Maddie was so excited she'd wanted to visit ''her'' puppy almost every day. Only by exerting great diplomacy had Janice been able to restrain her daughter to one visit per week.

Kim leaned back in her chair, knocking against the wall because there was so little room in her office. ''Jay called a while ago. He said Logan came back to work today.''

Janice's heart did a tumble, but she managed to keep a straight face. Obviously Kim knew Logan had rescued Janice's son from the fire. ''I'm glad to hear that.''

''Sounds like the guys coerced or bribed him into cooking his specialty right off.''

''Clam linguini,'' Janice acknowledged softly.

''He's also going to bake some apple pies.''

Intentionally, Janice continued to study the printouts in her hand. She didn't want to talk about Logan. Even the thought of him brought a terrible ache to her chest, so painful she had trouble breathing. She'd missed seeing him a thousand different ways. Even Kevin's soccer practices were depressing, knowing Logan wouldn't be there.

"If there was a firefighter I wanted to see," Kim said in a casual tone, "and I knew he was baking apple pies, I bet I'd buy a couple of gallons of ice cream and take it to the station house. Just to say thanks, you understand."

Looking up, Janice saw understanding in Kim's eyes—and sympathy. "Am I that transparent?"

"Seems to me that for a long time I thought something was going on between you two. Probably even before you knew it yourselves."

"While I was married, I never once—"

"I know that. No one has ever suggested an ounce of impropriety between you and Logan. But since Ray's death, maybe we thought something might, well, develop."

Oh, it had, on her part. But she still wasn't sure about Logan and how he felt.

"Why don't you take some ice cream over to the station tonight? I know Jay loves pie à la mode. The rest of the guys probably do, too."

For a moment, Janice rationalized she hadn't properly thanked any of the firefighters for their part in saving Kevin's life. Ice cream was the traditional way to celebrate any event in the fire department—a long-

standing custom. It would be reasonable for her to
drop by with a gallon or two.

Then she realized that was only an excuse for her
desperate need to see Logan, if only for a moment.

Chapter Fourteen

"You missed your calling, Strong." Danny Sullivan scooped up the very last drop of linguini from the second pan. "You should have been a French chef in one of those fancy restaurants."

"Linguini's Italian, bozo," Turrick piped up, grinning.

Logan had already cleaned his plate and was enjoying the way the men scrambled to get more than their fair share of the double recipe he'd concocted. "Maybe I ought to start charging you guys extra for my talents."

"No way!" Diaz said. "I've got too many mouths at home to feed."

"Where's that pie you promised?" Gables asked.

"Coming." Logan shoved himself to his feet.

"Would you like to have your pie à la mode?"

Every head in the room swiveled toward Janice, who stood in the doorway holding two grocery sacks. An instant later she was surrounded by firefighters, all eager to help carry her load.

"If we get a run now," Gables announced, snaring

a gallon of ice cream, "I don't care what building's on fire. As far as I'm concerned, it can burn to the ground—unless it's my own house, of course."

Everyone laughed.

Everyone except Logan. He couldn't even move. He was too stunned at seeing Janice, the spear of need and loneliness slicing through him so painfully he was barely able to breathe.

Letting the general chaos disguise his reaction, he stood back as the others swooped Janice into their midst, whirled her into the kitchen area where they sliced the pies and served them with big dollops of vanilla ice cream. She looked terrific. A summery skirt and a loose top, her dark curls casually framing her face. Her cheeks flushed with excitement, her soft laughter drifting through the room in contrast to the deeper voices of the men.

Logan couldn't keep his eyes off her, tracked her every movement, relished every sound she made.

When the others had been served and settled down to eat their pie and ice cream, Janice brought him a plate.

"Aren't you hungry?"

The only thing he was hungry for was Janice. "Thanks," he said, taking the plate.

Her soft, brown eyes studied him. "I heard you came back to work today."

"First day on the job."

"Then you're all right? Your hands?"

He showed her. "They're fine. How 'bout you and the kids?"

"We're good. My job's going well, too."

"That's good." They were dancing around each other, not touching, but checking for new boundaries, looking for the borders of their relationship since they'd backed away from being lovers. *One night.* That's all they'd had together.

"Well, I wanted to thank you…everyone. For rescuing Kevin, I mean. I thought they'd appreciate the ice cream."

"Sure." They both knew C-shift hadn't been on duty that day but it didn't seem to matter. "It's great."

"I guess I'd better be going."

Without having taken a bite of pie or ice cream, he set the plate on the table. "I'll walk you downstairs."

A faint smile lifted her lips. "I'd like that."

He let her go first. So he wouldn't touch her. So he could watch the sway of her hips, enjoy the subtle shifting of her hair at the back of her neck. Her sandals slapped on the stairs as they descended to the deserted bay where the fire trucks were all tucked in for the night, the lights dimmed.

She stopped at the back of Engine 61. "Did you ever see that movie *Back Draft?*"

"A long time ago."

Without looking at him, she said, "Ray used to tell me it was every firefighter's fantasy to make love to a woman on top of a fire truck like they did in the movie."

Logan swallowed hard. "I've always figured it would be darn uncomfortable—the hoses aren't exactly as soft as a mattress."

She turned to him with a little smile. "You've always been practical, haven't you?"

He was dumbstruck by the dark glimmer of need in her eyes, the same need that had been filling him for the past two weeks.

"Boost me up, Logan. We've both spent our lives being too practical."

Unable to refuse anything she asked of him, he moved in closer, his hands finding her slender waist. She smelled of flowers, as fresh as her garden, and he boosted her to the bumper, followed her up, then lifted her higher to sit on the coiled rows of hose.

His hands trembled, he felt unsteady. "Sometimes fantasy doesn't hold a candle to the real thing."

She leaned over, kissing him. He drank in her sweetness, tasted her hot, honeyed innocence. He craved more, a deeper intimacy, a sense of coming home. He heard her sigh, the whisper of his name on her lips, and tried not to let the urgency building within him go too far.

He felt himself teeter on the edge, not on the edge of the bumper but on the edge of lunacy. He actually wanted to crawl up there with her, make love to her on the top of a fire truck. His natural caution had gone up in smoke. He was incapable of resisting the temptation of holding Janice again. Of loving her.

His hand found its way beneath her blouse. He palmed the weight of her breast, toyed with the nipple that instantly puckered in his hand. Rejoiced in the yielding of her flesh against his.

He planted his foot on a valve to push himself up.

The overhead lights flashed on, blindingly bright.

"Strong? Are you in here?"

Logan swore, gave Janice a helpless look, then hopped down just as Chief Gray rounded the end of the truck.

The chief looked at Logan, then up at Janice and shook his head, though his eyes had started to twinkle. "I wish to goodness they hadn't made that damn movie."

Turning, Logan helped Janice down with as much aplomb as they could both muster, given the circumstances. Her cheeks were flaming red; his were just as hot.

"I'm sorry, chief—" she began.

He held up his hand to stop her apology. "I'm the one that should apologize for my timing, but I'm glad I caught you both. That is...not that I'm glad I caught you at this exact moment, you understand." Apparently as embarrassed as they were, he cleared his throat. "I've just come from a city council meeting, and I've got good news for both of you."

"News, sir?" Logan asked, forcing himself back to some semblance of sanity.

"The city council, in its collective wisdom, has overridden the Civil Service Commission test results, and my guess is that there's not a soul in the county who will object." He smiled at Logan. "Congratulations. You're number one on the promotion list."

It took a moment for Logan to process the chief's announcement. "For engineer?"

"Well, not for my job, young man. I figure I've got a few good years yet before retirement."

"Yes, sir, I mean—"

"Logan, that's wonderful!" Janice squeezed his hand, then remembering the chief had virtually caught them in the act, quickly let go. "Your father will be so proud of you."

"There's another thing you ought to know," the chief said before Logan had a chance to react. "The whole department, everyone who worked on Big Red, took a vote last week. They want you to be the one to drive her in the Founder's Day parade on Saturday."

Logan gawked at his boss. "Me?"

Winking at Janice, the chief said, "Maybe Strong's been playing those bagpipes too loud lately and it's made him go deaf."

"No, sir. I mean, I didn't think—"

The chief cut him off. "The city council asked me to extend an invitation to you, Mrs. Gainer, and your children to ride Big Red in the parade, too. They'd feel it an honor if you'd accept."

"Oh, Chief Gray—" Her eyes widened, and she looked as surprised as Logan had about being placed at the top of the promotion list. "That's very kind of…" She glanced at Logan, smiling. "The children will be so excited, particularly Kevin. And Maddie will be in seventh heaven."

"Good. That's decided." Harlan Gray slid his hands into his trouser pockets. "Seems to me I'm overdue at home, so I'll leave you two to...to whatever you were doing.''

Logan stood at attention until Chief Gray vanished through the door to the administrative offices and so did Janice. Then she burst into giggles.

"I can't believe he caught us," she said.

"Neither can I." In the most natural move he'd ever made, Logan pulled her into his arms. "I'm darn lucky he didn't fire me on the spot."

"What? The city council's top man on the promotion list? He wouldn't dare." She kissed him lightly. "Congratulations, Logan. You deserve that promotion."

Given that he'd missed the oral exam, he wasn't so sure about that. He did know what he wanted, however, and that was Janice. But not here. And—now that a certain amount of reason had returned to his senses—not until he found a job that wouldn't leave a woman terrified at the sound of every siren. Whenever she and her children were ready, he wanted Janice permanently—as his wife.

Framing her face between his hands, he kissed her again. "You'd better go, sweetheart. A man can only stand so much temptation. I'll be seeing you Saturday."

He watched her go out the back gate and waited until he heard the van pull away.

Despite the prospect of a promotion, he knew what he had to do. He hadn't been willing to give up firefighting for Torie, his first wife. Maybe he'd been too young. Or hadn't loved her enough.

Janice was different. For her, he'd surrender every dream he'd ever held.

A PERFECT California fall day greeted the residents of Paseo del Real for the annual Founder's Day parade. The cloudless sky was Wedgwood blue, the high temperature expected to be in the mid-sixties. Along the parade route, liquidambar trees mimicked maples in their coats of red and gold leaves. Families lined the sidewalks with strollers and folding chairs, kids sitting on the curbs; clowns hawked balloons while members of the VFW passed out tiny American flags.

Logan shifted into second, easing Big Red in behind the high-school band. He'd driven the old fire truck around the block a couple of times yesterday and knew the transmission tended to grind. Even so he winced, glancing at Janice sitting next to him.

Amused, she smiled back at him. "Tommy assured me you'd get the hang of it soon."

"Right. But he might want to take another auto shop class before he graduates."

Tommy and his girlfriend Rachel, a pretty little redhead with a face full of freckles, were sitting in the back of the truck, the young man shyly holding her hand.

Kevin and Maddie were there, too, in the center of the rig, Maddie in charge of Suzie and her puppies. A proud papa, Buttons had perched himself right behind Logan where he could survey the cheering crowd.

Jay Tolliver and Mike Gables had gotten themselves vintage fire fighter uniforms from the local historical society and were hanging onto the back of the truck. Meanwhile, their wives tossed hard candies to the kids along the parade route—at least the candy that Mike and Kristin's adopted son Randy hadn't yet eaten.

Keeping Big Red rolling at the walking pace of the band, Logan relaxed and enjoyed the excitement of the crowd…and the pleasure of Janice sitting next to him. The twinge of regret he felt knowing he'd soon give up the fire department for another, less risky job was something he could easily ignore. Or so he told himself as they approached the reviewing stand where the mayor, members of the city council and other dignitaries waited to salute them.

Kevin climbed up beside Buttons and stuck his head between Logan and Janice. He had his father's Medal of Valor hanging around his neck on a patriotic ribbon.

"This is really cool, huh?"

"It's an honor for all of us," Janice agreed.

"Hey, Logan, when are you and Mom gonna get married?"

The wheel jerked in Logan's hand, and he snapped his head around. "What?"

"Me 'n' Maddie have been talkin'. It doesn't take a genius to figure out Mom misses seeing you. So it makes sense you two oughta get married."

"Watch out!" Janice grabbed for the wheel. "You're about to run over the pedestrians."

Valiantly trying to keep himself as well as the fire truck under control, Logan turned back into line. "I haven't exactly proposed yet, Kevin."

"Why not?"

Janice cocked her brow at him, her eyes teasing. "Now there's an interesting question."

"Because I have some things to work out first."

Half draped into the front seat, Kevin waved at some of his school friends. "Like what?" he persisted.

Logan scowled. "Like finding a new job, that's what."

"You're kidding," Janice gasped. "Why on earth would you want to change jobs?"

Looking over his shoulder, Logan said, "Kevin, how 'bout you getting back where you belong so your mother and I can—"

"I'm not hurting anything," Kevin objected.

The kid was going to need some serious talking to, but at the moment Logan didn't have the time. He had to deal with Janice first. "I've begun looking for a different, safer job so you wouldn't have to sit home after we're married worrying about the fire chief showing up at the door a second time to announce your husband has died in the line of duty."

"But you're about to be promoted. After all this time, and what it means to you and your father, surely you don't want to give up the career you've worked so hard for?"

Kevin said, "Makes sense to me."

Logan ignored the boy. "I'd give up anything for you, including my job. I've already talked to a restaurant in Pismo Beach that's looking for a chef. It's an upscale—"

"No, absolutely not."

He braked hard. "What do you mean, no?"

"Geez!" Kevin nearly fell into his mother's lap. "Take it easy, Logan!"

Janice helped her son back up. "I mean, don't you dare give up the job you love—"

"I love cooking, too."

"—because you're afraid I might worry about you on the job. Being a firefighter is what you do, who you are."

"I play bagpipes, too, but that doesn't mean—"

"Logan Strong, I have no intention of forcing you to sacrifice your family traditions, any of them, just to marry me. Your father might be able to forgive me if I allowed that to happen, but I'd never be able to forgive myself."

Someone yelled at Logan to get the truck going again. The gears protested as he shifted into first and accelerated, lurching the fire engine forward.

"Does that mean you *want* to marry me?"

"Of course I do. I thought that must have been pretty obvious in Las Vegas."

"You don't think it's too soon? I mean, it's only been a few months—"

"I don't think there's a time limit on how long it takes to fall in love."

"How 'bout getting married at Thanksgiving?" Kevin asked, his head right between them again. "Then me and Maddie could go on the honeymoon with you."

Both Logan and Janice whirled around to glare at her son.

"Don't even think about it," Janice said sternly.

"Not a chance," Logan agreed.

A scream went up from the reviewing stand.

Logan turned to see city officials scrambling to get out of the way of Big Red. He slammed on the brakes. The truck shuddered, the engine died and came to a stop inches from the temporary bleachers set up for the dignitaries.

Hands trembling for more than one reason, Logan exhaled slowly.

"What in the name of heaven do you think you're doing?" Chief Gray bellowed. He was standing on the third riser of the reviewing stand, his arms thrown protectively around Councilwoman Anderson, his stance and uniform suggestive of a knight determined to slay a dragon for his queen, or die trying.

"I'm sorry, sir," Logan muttered. "I, ah, just proposed to Janice—I think—and she accepted—I think. I sort of lost track—"

"Oh, Harlan, isn't that romantic?" The councilwoman resettled her glasses, which apparently had been dislodged during all the excitement. Quite large and tinted blue, amazingly they went well with her gray hair and added a dramatic flair to her appearance.

"Romantic or not, Evie dear, one of my men almost ran over the members of the entire city council. That could cost me my job."

"Not as long as I have a vote, sweet'ums," she crooned.

Nearly choking herself, Janice swallowed a laugh. "Maybe you ought to see if you can get this thing started again so we can finish the parade."

That seemed the wisest course. So Logan cranked the engine over, shifted into reverse, which sent a Western riding club on horseback behind him into disarray, then aimed Big Red down the boulevard again.

He'd proposed. Janice had accepted. And it was okay with Kevin. He thought. But there were a few details that had yet to be worked out.

ONCE BACK at Station Six, Logan took Janice by the hand and forcefully dragged her upstairs to his quarters. Granted, he wasn't on duty, but it was the only place he could think of where they could be alone.

"The children?" she protested.

"The guys will take care of them." He shoved the door closed behind him, whirled around, grabbed Janice none too gently and kissed her. Long and hard and more deeply than he should until things were settled. With an effort he broke the kiss. "Do you want to marry me?"

"*If* you love me—"

"Oh, yes, more than I can possibly tell you."

"—and assuming you know I'm not going to *sit* anywhere waiting for anything. I have a job and I have no intention of giving that up."

"How 'bout taking time out for more babies?"

Going very still inside, Janice was stunned and thrilled by his question. She'd always dreamed of a big family, more babies to hold and cuddle. "Do you mean it?"

"Only if you want more. Kevin and Maddie are terrific. I wouldn't have any trouble—"

"I want to have your babies. Lots of them."

He grinned. "A couple will do."

"And you won't give up your job with the department?" She couldn't bear the thought of him making that big a sacrifice for her.

"Not unless you want me to. Then I'd do it in a nanosecond."

Her heart nearly filling her throat, she caressed his cheek with her hand. "I love you, Logan Strong."

"I love you, too." He bent to kiss her—

Someone pounded on the door.

Abruptly, Logan yanked it open. "What?"

Kevin lifted his shoulders in a careless shrug. "I figured, if you're gonna be my new dad and stuff…would it be okay if I slid down the pole now?"

He shot a glance at Janice, who was fighting to keep a smile in check. "It's still your decision," he said, "but I think he's old enough."

Janice nodded her approval. It was time she let her son grow up and find his own independence, as she had discovered hers.

Pumping his fist in the air, Kevin shouted, "Yes!" and dashed away, only to be replaced in the doorway by Maddie, her eyes big and hopeful. "Me, too?"

Logan scooped her up in his arms. "Not quite yet, sprite, at least not on your own."

"Can I go down with you?" she asked solemnly.

He checked with Janice again. "Tell you what. Why don't the three of us go down together."

"I couldn't," Janice gasped.

"Sure you can." He held out his arm and, with only

a slight hesitation, she joined him. The spirit of adventure bubbled inside her.

Holding Maddie tight in one arm, he instructed Janice on how to grasp the pole. When she grabbed hold, he did too, and together the three of them stepped off into a new life, a new world of love.

Janice reached ground level breathless and flushed, exhilarated by a sense of accomplishment.

Applause erupted from the dozens of firefighters hanging around, those on duty and those who'd been in the parade.

Emma Jean clapped the loudest. "I knew you two would get together eventually. I saw it in my crystal ball. I even predicted it at Mike Gables's wedding," she said smugly.

"Okay, if you're so psychic," Logan said, looping his arm around Janice's waist while he still held tight to Maddie, "who's the next bachelor destined to bite the dust?"

The dispatcher scanned the room, her full red lips lifting in a smile as she tilted her head, making her jewelry jingle. "It might take a while."

"Yeah, right," Danny Sullivan taunted. "You're hedging, Emma Jean. You can't see the future at all."

"I can't?" she questioned, and there was something sly in her dark gypsy eyes. "An Irishman like you ought to know the power of romance."

Given that she'd seen what Logan had been blind to, he wasn't going to question Emma Jean's psychic abilities. He was simply going to get on with his life with Janice at his side, along with the family he'd always dreamed about having.

He pulled Janice close again. "I love you," he whispered.

She mouthed "I love you too," and that was all he needed to know.

* * * * *

Charlotte Maclay's

MEN OF STATION SIX

continues with Danny Sullivan's story in 2002, only from Harlequin American Romance.

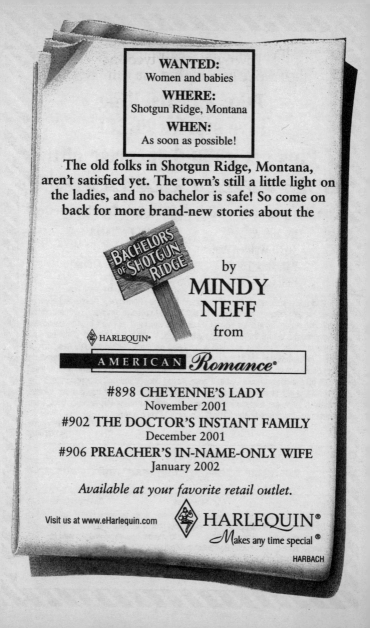

If you enjoyed what you just read,
then we've got an offer you can't resist!

Take 2 bestselling
love stories FREE!
Plus get a FREE surprise gift!

CALL THE ONES YOU LOVE OVER THE HOLIDAYS!

Save $25 off future book purchases when you buy any four Harlequin® or Silhouette® books in October, November and December 2001,

PLUS

receive a phone card good for 15 minutes of long-distance calls to anyone you want in North America!

WHAT AN INCREDIBLE DEAL!

Just fill out this form and attach 4 proofs of purchase (cash register receipts) from October, November and December 2001 books, and Harlequin Books will send you a coupon booklet worth a total savings of $25 off future purchases of Harlequin® and Silhouette® books, AND a 15-minute phone card to call the ones you love, anywhere in North America.

Please send this form, along with your cash register receipts as proofs of purchase, to:
In the USA: Harlequin Books, P.O. Box 9057, Buffalo, NY 14269-9057
In Canada: Harlequin Books, P.O. Box 622, Fort Erie, Ontario L2A 5X3
Cash register receipts must be dated no later than December 31, 2001.
Limit of 1 coupon booklet and phone card per household.
Please allow 4-6 weeks for delivery.

I accept your offer! Please send me my coupon booklet and a 15-minute phone card:

Name: _____

Address: _____ City: _____

State/Prov.: _____ Zip/Postal Code: _____

Account Number (if available): _____

---

097 KJB DAGL
PHQ4012